"Don't Push Me Away, Amanda," Michael Said.

"It was just a kiss," she said, deliberately sounding flip. "Let's not make it into more than it was."

Michael stiffened. Just a kiss? It was a lot more than that, and they both knew it. He wasn't going to let her get away so easily. Amanda retrieved her house keys from her purse, and Michael took them from her fingers. Unlocking the door, he pushed it open.

"Aren't you going to ask me in?"

"No," she said primly. "I'm not."

"Then next time."

"There won't be any next time." She tipped up her chin.

The haughtiness of her tone caused Michael to snap. Before he could stop himself, he reached for her. Cupping the back of her head, he pulled her to him.

"I promise you, Amanda, there will be a next time. Tonight was only the beginning."

Dear Reader,

I know this is a hectic time of year. From the moment you cut into that Thanksgiving turkey, to the second midnight chimes on December 31, life is one nonstop *RUSH*. But don't forget to take some private time…and relax with Silhouette Desire!

We begin with *An Obsolete Man*, a marvelous *Man of the Month* from the ever-entertaining Lass Small. Next we have *The Headstrong Bride*, the latest installment in Joan Johnston's CHILDREN OF HAWK'S WAY series.

And there's *Hometown Wedding*, the first book in a fun-filled new series, JUST MARRIED, by Pamela Macaluso, a talented new-to-Desire writer. And speaking of new authors, don't miss Metsy Hingle's debut title, *Seduced*.

This month is completed with *Dark Intentions*, a sensuous, heartwarming love story by Carole Buck, and *Murdock's Family*, a powerfully dramatic offering by Paula Detmer Riggs.

Happy holidays—don't worry, you'll survive them!

Lucia Macro
Senior Editor

Please address questions and book requests to:
Silhouette Reader Service
U.S.: 3010 Walden Ave., P.O. Box 1325, Buffalo, NY 14269
Canadian: P.O. Box 609, Fort Erie, Ont. L2A 5X3

METSY
HINGLE
SEDUCED

SILHOUETTE *Desire*®
Published by Silhouette Books
America's Publisher of Contemporary Romance

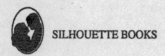 SILHOUETTE BOOKS

ISBN 0-373-05900-0

SEDUCED

Copyright © 1994 by Metsy Hingle

METSY HINGLE

is a native of New Orleans who loves the city in which she grew up. She credits the charm, antiquity and decadence of her birthplace, along with the passionate nature of her own French heritage, with instilling in her the desire to write. Married and the mother of four children, she believes in romance and happy endings. Becoming a Silhouette author is a long-cherished dream come true for Metsy and one happy ending that she continues to celebrate with each new story she writes.

For Jim,
my husband, my lover, my friend

Prologue

"**A**shes to ashes, dust to dust..."

Michael Grayson could barely make out the words of the muffled prayer as the priest's voice broke and faded in the brisk January wind.

"We commend our sister to you, Lord..."

Sister. Michael swallowed as he caught the word. He stared at the coffin. Rose petals escaped from the floral wreath positioned nearby and scattered across the ivory casket, creating bright splotches of color in the bleak New Orleans cemetery.

"Now that she has passed from this life..."

He glanced down at his seven-year-old niece. Dressed in the navy blue wool coat and white leggings he'd purchased for her a few days earlier, Summer stood dry-eyed and silent beside him. A strong gust swept over the grave site and she shivered. Michael moved behind her to block the wind.

"May she live on in your presence, oh, Lord..."

Michael shifted his gaze to the waiting tomb... the dark, lifeless crypt where Sara's body would soon rest.

Sara. His beautiful, free-spirited, younger sister. Michael squeezed his eyes shut. Images of Sara—laughing, painting, holding baby Summer in her arms—raced across his shuttered lids like frames from a movie projector. The pictures slowed, stopping on his last memory of Sara—her face filled with defiance and fear. She'd been afraid when she'd left. For Summer, for herself, for him.

After six long years she'd come home—in a coffin. And Summer... He opened his eyes and looked down at his niece. Summer had returned a stranger—to him and to the Western world.

"In your mercy and love, forgive whatever sins she may have committed..."

The attendants moved the granite slab away from the vault entrance. Michael took a deep breath. The ache that had taken root deep inside him when the call had come from India spread.

"Grant her eternal rest, oh, Lord..."

"Uncle Mike?"

At the tug on his hand, Michael looked down into a pair of familiar green eyes—eyes identical to those that had viewed him and his family with such coldness, eyes he'd learned to hate.

"Uncle Mike," Summer whispered again.

Michael shook his head to clear the image. Guilt surged through him as he studied the pale, heart-shaped face of his niece. She's a Grayson, he reminded himself, dropping down on one knee. "What is it, sweetheart?"

"Who's that lady?" She pointed to a tall woman standing across from them. "She's staring at me."

Michael looked past the circle of mourners and sucked in an angry breath as his eyes locked with Martha Winthrop's. Even with the dark fur hat shadowing her face, he recognized the avaricious gleam in Martha's green eyes. Regal in her full-length ranch mink coat, she gave no indication of her sixty-eight years or the heart of ice she possessed.

"Nobody important," Michael said, slanting a glance to the slender blond man standing beside Martha. He watched as Bradley Winthrop leaned closer and whispered something to his aunt.

"She *looks* important. Maybe she was a friend of my mother's."

"No," Michael said, his voice sharper than he'd intended. "She's not a friend."

Moments later the service ended. After thanking the priest and small gathering of friends who had come to pay their respects, Michael looked one last time at the tomb. Turning away, he took Summer's hand and headed toward the waiting limousine. When he reached the car, the chauffeur opened the rear door. "Give me a minute," he told the dark-suited driver, and the man obediently retreated.

Stooping down, Michael brushed a tangle of dark curls behind Summer's left ear. "Honey, you do understand that your mother's . . . gone, don't you?"

"You mean, she's dead," Summer said matter-of-factly.

"Yes." Once again, he marveled at the child's calm acceptance of her mother's death.

"Michael."

Michael stiffened at the sound of Martha Winthrop's voice. Slowly he rose to his feet and drew Summer to his side.

"I was sorry to hear about Sara's accident."

"Were you?" Michael asked, making no attempt to hide his bitterness.

Martha's lips tightened, etching deep lines at the corners of her mouth, but her voice was cool, controlled. "Despite what you believe, I never wished your sister any ill will."

"No. Not as long as she stayed away from your precious son."

"If you'll recall, I did offer to help her before she ran off."

"You mean you tried to buy her off! And when that didn't work, you used threats. If I had known—"

"That's enough, Grayson!" Bradley took a step toward Michael.

"Stop it," Martha commanded. "You'll frighten the child."

Bradley stilled, but his eyes flashed dangerously. Michael could almost smell the other man's anger.

Martha glared openly at both men before turning toward Summer. "Don't pay any attention to them, dear," she said gently. "I'm Martha Winthrop and you must be Summer." She held out her gloved hand.

Summer hesitated. She looked from Martha to Michael and back again. Tentatively, she shook Martha's hand. "You were staring at me," she said.

A flicker of surprise crossed Martha's face. "Yes. I suppose I was."

"Why?"

"Probably because I was so glad to see you again." Martha stooped down in front of Summer and touched her cheek. "You were such a little thing the last time I saw you. You're even prettier now than I remembered."

"You know me?"

"Yes."

"Did you know my mother, too?"

"Yes, dear." Martha smiled. "I knew both of your parents."

She shot Michael a triumphant look and he fought the urge to strangle the woman.

"I'm hoping now that you've come home, you and I can become friends. Would you like that?"

Anger and the beginnings of fear raced through Michael. He grabbed Summer's hand. "Come on, Summer. We have to go." He ushered her inside the car and shut the door, then turned back to Martha. "I'm warning you. Stay away from her. There's no place in Summer's life for you or any Winthrop."

"I have rights, Michael," she whispered. Her voice dropped lower. "Or need I remind you that she's my—"

"*She's* a Grayson." Michael took a menacing step toward her. "You may have been able to frighten my sister, but I don't scare so easily. If you come within so much as a mile of her..." He shot a glance at Bradley. "Either of you—I swear, I'll make you wish you'd never been born."

Before she could respond, Michael marched over to the other side of the car and jerked open the door. He slid onto the seat beside Summer. As they pulled away from the cemetery, he looked in the side-view mirror. He recognized the determination in Martha's expression.

Gradually the figures grew smaller in the distance as the car moved slowly down the road. Curling his hands into fists, Michael looked over at his silent niece. *Don't worry, Sara. I'll never let her have Summer. Never.*

One

How did the kid do it? Michael wondered as he stepped inside the reception area of Saint Margaret's Grade School. How could one pint-size little girl manage to get into so much trouble?

Quickly he took in the familiar surroundings—the wall lined with file cabinets, bulletin boards crammed with colored bits of paper, an ever-changing assortment of parents and students waiting to meet with counselors and teachers. He glanced over at the closed doors leading to the offices of the principal and the school's administrative staff.

Bracing himself, he moved across the worn, beige tile and tried to ignore the annoying hum of the fluorescent lights overhead.

The silver-haired receptionist greeted him with a smile. "Can I help you?" she asked in a voice as thick and sweet as molasses.

"I'm Michael Grayson. Sister Mary Grace is expecting me."

"I thought I recognized you, Mr. Grayson. You were here last week to see Sister Mary Grace, weren't you?"

"Yes, I was." The truth was, he'd been to the principal's office four times in the six weeks since he had enrolled Summer.

"I thought so," she said, obviously pleased at her recognitive ability. "You're little Summer's father."

"Uncle," he corrected. Impatient, he looked at the closed door to the principal's office again. "I'd appreciate your letting Sister know that I'm here."

"Of course, but I'm afraid she's running a bit behind schedule today. She shouldn't be too much longer, though. You can have a seat if you'd like." She gestured toward the row of metal chairs positioned along the wall. Two chairs were occupied by students who looked a bit green around the gills. A third seat was taken by a woman resembling Florence Henderson on the old "Brady Bunch" sitcom who was busily chatting with a pregnant brunette.

Michael eyed the two remaining seats. They looked small and uncomfortable. "Thanks, but I think I'll just stand," he said, feeling extremely large and decidedly out of place.

"I guess you're here because of Summer's problem in Mrs. Green's class this morning," the receptionist said.

Michael snapped to attention. "What problem?"

Amanda Bennett winced at the edge in his voice as she watched the exchange from the doorway.

So this is Michael Grayson.

Amanda took in the crop of dark hair, the navy jacket that spanned his wide shoulders, the large hands braced on the reception desk. One of the younger teachers had described him as a "hunk... Six foot plus of muscle and sex appeal." Seeing him for the first time, she could understand the other woman's reaction.

"Oh, my." The receptionist's face turned a bright pink. "I assumed Sister Mary Grace had told you..."

"Told me what?" he demanded.

Obviously, the "hunk" had a temper, Amanda thought, frowning. She studied the stiff lines of his body, his thunderous expression. And Gracie expected *her* to persuade *him* to allow his niece to participate in the school's counseling program?

"I mean, I thought that was the reason you were here... because of what happened."

He loomed over the desk and glared at the receptionist; the woman paled under his ferocious scowl.

No, Amanda decided. Michael Grayson definitely didn't look like the kind of man one "persuaded" to do anything. In fact, she suspected he did exactly what he wanted to do, when he wanted to do it.

"Why don't you just tell me exactly what happened," he commanded.

"I—"

"Mrs. Evans," Amanda said, stepping forward. "I believe Sister Mary Grace can see Mr. Grayson now."

The other woman's shoulders slumped in obvious relief as Michael Grayson swung his angry gaze from the nervous Mrs. Evans to her. At the sight of those flashing blue eyes, Amanda immediately wondered at her wisdom in rescuing the older woman.

His gaze skimmed the length of her and suddenly Amanda felt as though her tailored lemon suit was much too daring.

Dismissing her reaction as foolish, Amanda tipped up her chin. "If you'll come with me, Mr. Grayson, I'll show you in to Sister Mary Grace." Without waiting for his response, she turned and started toward the principal's office.

To Amanda, the few yards to Gracie's office seemed like a mile with *him* walking behind her. She could almost feel his eyes trained on her back, watching her movements. She tapped on the door.

"I didn't catch your name, Miss..."

Amanda turned to look at him and swallowed when she found him so close. She fought the urge to step back. "Bennett. Amanda Bennett," she said, her voice more breathless than she would have liked.

"Come in," Gracie called out.

Relieved at the prospect of putting distance between them, Amanda opened the door and entered the room. Michael followed.

"Mr. Grayson." The tiny nun came bustling from behind her desk, a flurry of energy in a religious habit.

"Sister." Michael shook her hand.

"I see you've already met Amanda," Sister Mary Grace said.

"Yes, I have." Cutting a glance to her, Michael smiled.

The simple movement of his lips—slight though it was—softened the harsh lines of his face, warmed the coolness of those blue eyes. Amanda's pulse skittered in response.

"And of course, you know Mrs. Green." Sister Mary Grace gestured toward the woman seated in front of the desk.

Michael's smile dissolved immediately. "Mrs. Green."

Yes, Amanda decided, confirming her initial impression. Michael Grayson was definitely going to be difficult. She could only hope that if he loved his niece as much as Gracie seemed to think he did, he would listen to reason.

"Why don't you have a seat?" Sister Mary Grace motioned to the chair beside Mrs. Green's. When the nun had resumed her own seat, Amanda slipped into the chair adjacent to the desk so that she could observe him.

"I know how busy you are, and I appreciate your coming so quickly," Sister Mary Grace began. "I wish all of our parents were as responsive as you."

"Anything concerning my niece is important to me, Sister. What seems to be the problem?"

"The problem, Mr. Grayson, is that your niece insists on disrupting my class," Frances Green informed him.

"Frances, please," Sister Mary Grace admonished.

Michael narrowed his eyes. "And just how did she manage to disrupt your class this time, Mrs. Green?"

His voice was soft. Too soft, Amanda thought, noting the rigid line of his jaw.

"Well, for starters, she pretended to go into a trance in the middle of my lesson, and then she—"

"A trance?" Michael repeated.

"Not a trance," Amanda corrected, noting the way his fingers had tightened around the arms of the chair. "She was meditating."

"Call it whatever you like," Frances Green countered, her too thin shoulders stiff with indignation. "All I know is the child kept staring off into space, pretending she couldn't hear me."

Michael gritted his teeth. He hadn't thought it possible to dislike the sour-faced teacher more, but he did. "Maybe she didn't hear you," Michael offered. He certainly wouldn't blame Summer if she had pretended not to hear the woman.

"Oh, she could hear me, all right. Why, if it hadn't been for Amanda..."

Amanda?

Michael moved his gaze from Mrs. Green to the blonde, trying once more to place her name and face among those staff members he'd met at the last PTA meeting. He took in the waterfall of blond hair, the trim waist and long legs. She had great legs, he thought, unable to resist looking at them again. No, Amanda Bennett hadn't been at the PTA meeting. If she had, he would certainly have remembered her.

"...And that awful humming sound she kept making," Mrs. Green continued.

"Mantras," Amanda explained.

He caught the New England accent again and his curiosity escalated another notch.

"Whatever," Mrs. Green said. "All I know is that it gave me goose bumps."

Pulling his attention back to Mrs. Green, Michael half listened as the woman droned on. He'd heard a similar tale last week when Summer had brought the talisman to school.

Frustrated, Michael wanted to demand once again that Summer be transferred to another class. But any such demand was pointless. Frances Green was the only religion teacher for the third grade. And if he wanted Summer to remain at Saint Margaret's—and he did—she had to take the class.

"As I've explained to Sister Mary Grace, I have nothing against your niece, Mr. Grayson. But these disruptions she's causing are affecting the other students."

"I'll speak to Summer, Mrs. Green. You have my word, it won't happen again," he assured her, biting back his frustration for Summer's sake.

"Thank you, Frances," Sister Mary Grace said. "You can return to your students now."

The birdlike woman stood primly. "Thank you, Sister. Amanda." She inclined her head toward him. "Mr. Grayson."

Michael nodded, still too irritated by the woman's lack of empathy to even speak. Didn't she realize what Summer had been through? The death of her mother? The adjustments she had had to make? He swallowed. Hell, *he* still hadn't gotten over the loss of his sister. And he wasn't a vulnerable seven-year-old. He glared at the teacher's retreating back.

"Don't be too hard on Frances," Sister Mary Grace said after the woman had left the room. "She really is an excellent teacher, and she cares about her students."

"I'm sure you'd be a better judge of that than I would, Sister. At any rate, I'm sorry about what happened today. It's my fault for allowing Summer to continue the meditation at home. Obviously that was a mistake. One that I intend to rectify."

Amanda looked at Sister Mary Grace, then back at Michael. "Forgive me, Mr. Grayson. I realize this isn't any of my concern, but given Summer's background, do you think it's wise to discourage her from meditating?"

"You're right, Miss Bennett. It isn't any of your concern."

He heard the nun draw in a sharp breath and Michael realized he'd gone too far. But before he could apologize, Amanda was shooting back.

"That may be, but considering all that she's been through and the adjustments she's having to make, your taking a hard line on her meditation now could prove damaging."

"You seem to know a great deal about my niece, Miss Bennett," he said, suspicious.

"She and I spent some time together after this morning's incident. We talked for a while."

"I see," he said in a voice that was deliberately calm. He didn't like the idea of Summer being questioned by anyone, particularly about her background. Questions had a way of leading to more questions. And some questions were best left unanswered. "And based on a few minutes of conversation, you think you're in a better position to judge what's right for my niece than I am?"

She didn't so much as twitch an eyebrow. "Perhaps I am. Perhaps not. But then, I hardly think six weeks as a guardian constitutes *your* being an authority."

Michael frowned, wondering once more exactly who Amanda Bennett was and why she was so interested in his niece. "Obviously, Summer wasn't the only one who confided in you." He glanced over at the silent nun.

Before Sister Mary Grace could speak, Amanda rushed on. "I assure you, Sister only spoke to me out of concern for your niece."

"Listen, Miss Bennett, I don't—"

"Actually, it's Dr. Bennett," Amanda informed him.

Michael narrowed his eyes. "Doctor?"

"Amanda's a child psychologist," Sister Mary Grace explained. "She works with some of the children here at the school. Naturally, I called her when Frances told me what had happened."

"I didn't realize Saint Margaret's employed a child psychologist on its staff," Michael said, making no attempt to keep the coldness from his voice.

"It doesn't," Amanda countered.

"Heavens, no," Sister Mary Grace added. "Saint Margaret's could never afford to pay for Amanda's services. We're simply grateful that she's willing to give us a few afternoons each week."

"That's very admirable of you, Dr. Bennett."

"Not at all," she returned in equally cool tones. "Since I'm not yet licensed to practice in Louisiana, volunteering at Saint Margaret's allows me to keep my feet wet while I study for the state exam. Besides, I find the work gratifying.''

"As Frances told you, Amanda was a tremendous help to us this morning," Sister Mary Grace added. "She's the one who brought Summer out of the meditative state."

Michael cut her a glance. "It seems I'm in your debt, Dr. Bennett."

"Not at all. I was glad I could help."

"Given the circumstances, I took the liberty of discussing the problems Summer's been having in school with Amanda," Sister Mary Grace informed him. "I thought it might help to get a professional's perspective. I hope you don't mind."

But he did mind—and very much. Forcing his voice to remain even, he said, "Sister, I know you meant well, but don't you think you're jumping the gun? I mean, just because Summer's had a few problems adjusting to the school doesn't mean she needs a child psychologist."

"What would you consider reason enough?" Amanda asked.

Michael tensed. He could feel the muscle twitch in his left cheek. "To be honest, I can't think of any reason Summer would need a shrink." They certainly hadn't helped his sister, he added silently.

Amanda bristled. She'd heard the term often enough, and there was no reason why having Michael Grayson call her by the unflattering name should bother her. But it did.

Sister Mary Grace sighed. "I'm sorry you feel that way, Mr. Grayson. I had hoped that perhaps with Amanda's help, we would have been able to allow Summer to remain at Saint Margaret's."

Michael froze. "What do you mean? Why wouldn't Summer be able to continue at Saint Margaret's?"

Amanda narrowed her eyes. What was Gracie up to? she wondered. She'd said she wanted help in convincing him to allow his niece to receive counseling. But nothing had been said about dismissing the child if their plan failed.

"Mr. Grayson…Michael," Sister Mary Grace amended. "I had Frances Green speak to you because I wanted you to see what you're up against. Saint Margaret's has a rigid teaching structure bound in Catholicism. And as you know, Summer's been exposed to a great many other cultures and beliefs—beliefs that are very much at odds with what she's being taught here."

"I know that, Sister. But Summer will adapt."

Sister Mary Grace shook her head. "I don't think so. At least, not without help."

"You and I have discussed this before, Sister. I'm not interested in putting Summer in any kind of therapy. She doesn't need it. All she needs is some time to adjust."

"She needs more than time, Michael. She needs help. I know you were opposed to the idea of counseling when I first suggested it. But I had hoped that after meeting Amanda and learning that Summer could work with her, here at the school, you might reconsider."

"I don't have to reconsider. The answer's no."

"Then you leave me no alternative. I have to consider what's best for the child and, under the circumstances, I honestly don't believe Saint Margaret's is good for Summer."

Michael sat forward, his face a mask of disbelief. "What are you saying?"

Amanda couldn't believe what she was hearing. "Really, Gracie—"

"I'm saying that I think it would be in Summer's best interests if you were to transfer her to another school. One that's less structured in its teaching matter, particularly where religion is concerned."

"Sister, you can't mean that," Michael said.

"I assure you I do."

"But don't you realize what affect this will have on Summer? She's never known any stability. Until now, her life has been nothing but a series of moves, from one city, one village, one country to the next. If I take her out of Saint Margaret's, it's just one more change. There've already been too many."

The anguish in his voice surprised Amanda. He seemed so strong, so defiant, not the kind of man who pleaded for anything. And yet he *was* pleading—for his niece's sake. "He's right," Amanda told her friend. "More changes wouldn't be good for the child."

"Neither will more incidents like today's." Sister Mary Grace leaned back in her chair and fingered the silver cross that hung from the chain around her neck. She looked at Amanda then at Michael. "Of course, if you were to reconsider and allow Summer to work with Amanda, if I knew she would be receiving professional guidance that would help her to deal with these adjustments she's having to make where the school's curriculum is concerned, I suppose it would be okay for her to remain at Saint Margaret's."

Amanda flushed. "Gra—"

"Well, Michael?"

Michael scowled. He curled his hands into fists. "It doesn't look like I have much choice. Do I?" But before Sister Mary Grace could respond, he conceded. "Never mind. What do I have to do to get Summer in the program?"

Sister Mary Grace stood, a smile spreading across her face. "Good. Then I'll leave it to Amanda to explain the details of the program to you and to work out a schedule for Summer."

Moments later, seated across from Amanda in the tiny office the school had designated for her use, Michael tried to squelch his irritation at having allowed a five-foot-nothing nun to outmaneuver him. It had been a long time since anyone had forced him into a corner this way. Not since the Winthrops—

Suddenly thoughts of Martha Winthrop and her demands to see Summer came back to him. Would the woman be able to use Summer's being in therapy against him? If she could, then maybe it would be better to transfer Summer to another school.

No. He wouldn't do that, he decided, pushing the thought aside. He'd been honest with Sister Mary Grace. Another change would be bad for Summer. He couldn't put her through that. But what if...

"Mr. Grayson?"

Michael jerked his attention back to Amanda.

"Are you all right?"

"Yeah. No." He rubbed the back of his neck, trying to ease the tense muscles. "Listen, do you think we could go somewhere and get a cup of coffee or something while we do this?"

Amanda eyed him warily. "I'm sorry, but I have another appointment in thirty minutes. Besides, I don't usually conduct meetings outside of the office."

"What about the school cafeteria?"

He read the no in her eyes, but before she could issue it, Michael added, "This hasn't exactly been a blue-ribbon day for me. And as I'm sure Sister Mary Grace has told you, I've spent a lot more time in these school offices during the past few weeks than most of the kids here. Now it looks like I'm going to be spending even more. I'll answer your questions and you can tell me about your program, but can't we do it someplace other than this office?"

"I'm sorry, Mr. Grayson, but I—"

"Michael," he corrected. "Come on, Amanda. All I'm asking is for you to cut me some slack. What do you say?"

She hesitated. "Well, I guess it would be okay for us to go to the teachers' lounge. It's not usually busy at this time of the day."

A few minutes later in the more relaxed setting, Michael had succeeded in reining in the panic that had threatened to swamp him earlier.

"As Sister Mary Grace told you, I've been working with a number of the students here and have attained a certain degree of success. Right now, I'm working with six other..."

Half listening as she explained the merits of the counseling program, Michael allowed the soothing sound of her voice to wash over him.

"...And while I know you're not happy about Summer participating in the program..."

He studied Amanda, noting her cool, efficient manner, her chic clothing. Everything about the woman—from the understated but expensive jewelry to the cultured tone of her voice—screamed "class" with a capital C. So why was she wasting her time in New Orleans counseling kids for nothing instead of hobnobbing with the rich and powerful back east?

What difference did it make? As long as it would make Sister Mary Grace happy and keep Summer at Saint Margaret's, that's all that mattered to him. Besides, it wasn't as if Summer really needed a shrink, he told himself. She didn't. And who knows, maybe the lovely Dr. Bennett could actually help him later. In fact, if he did find himself in a custody battle with Martha Winthrop, it certainly wouldn't hurt to have someone with Amanda's credentials in his corner.

"...And while I can't make any promises, I can assure you I'll do my best..."

His gaze slid from her sculptured features to her generous mouth. Colored a soft pink, her lips looked infinitely soft and inviting. He shook his head, surprised by the direction of his thoughts. "I'm sorry. What did you say?"

She shot him a puzzled look. "I said that I'd like to meet with you for a few minutes after my sessions with Summer so we can compare notes and discuss any concerns or changes in her behavior."

"All right."

"I generally schedule appointments between one-thirty and five. Is there any particular time that would be best for you?"

"The later, the better. Summer's in after-school care here at Saint Margaret's. I usually pick her up a little before six."

"Suppose I make Summer my last appointment at, say, five o'clock on Wednesdays and Fridays. That way, she and I will be finished just before you get here and then the two of us can meet."

"You need to see her twice a week?" Michael asked.

"I'd like to, at least at the start. We can always adjust the length and number of sessions later, depending on her progress." She paused. "Is that all right with you?"

"Yeah, I guess so. As long as you understand that these therapy sessions are just a trial thing. I mean, if they upset Summer or she doesn't seem to be responding, then they stop—regardless of what Sister Mary Grace does."

"I understand."

After jotting down the time and date in his appointment book, Michael slipped it into the inside pocket of his jacket.

Maybe Amanda Bennett really would be able to help, he told himself. Heaven knew, he hadn't been successful in erasing that haunted look that came into Summer's eyes whenever she spoke of her mother or asked questions about her father and his family.

"Well, then, if you don't have any other questions, I'll see you next week." Amanda stood and held out her hand.

Standing, Michael clasped her fingers in his. He paused and took in her lovely face, the graceful line of her neck, the way the yellow-and-white suit skimmed her full curves. Something stirred inside him that had nothing to do with her being a psychologist and everything to do with her being a woman and him being a man.

When he brought his gaze back to her face, her eyes had warmed to the color of sherry. A tiny sound escaped her lips before she pulled her hand free.

Michael hesitated, feeling a sudden reluctance to leave. "You know, despite my feelings about Summer being in therapy, I really do appreciate your helping her." He flashed her a smile and before he realized it, he said, "In fact, if you'll allow me to, I'd like to take you to dinner tonight to thank you. That is, if you're free."

"No, I'm not," she lied.

"Sure. I understand." He paused. "What about tomorrow?"

"Sorry, I can't."

"This weekend?" he persisted.

Turning away from the glimmer of interest in his eyes and her own foolish urge to accept, Amanda picked up the folder she'd placed on the table and clutched it to her. "I appreciate the offer, but I make it a rule never to mix business with pleasure. Now, if you'll excuse me, my next appointment should be waiting."

Moving past him, Amanda hurried out the door, her heart pounding loudly in her chest. The last thing she needed or wanted was a man like Michael Grayson. There was no room in her life for any man who came as part of a package deal—even one as appealing as Michael. Recalling the flicker of heat she had experienced when their eyes had met, Amanda squashed her traitorous thoughts. She'd learned her lesson the hard way. And she had no intention of repeating past mistakes.

Two

Two

—

"This isn't working, Amanda." Michael paced the length of the small school office. "It's been almost two months and Summer's still having the same problems. I'm pulling her out of the therapy program."

Amanda's heart lurched as she stared at Michael's stiff back. Despite all her silent lectures and resolutions not to become involved, both the man and the child had become important to her. "Michael, you can't do that. Not now. Not when she's starting to make progress."

He spun around, pinning her with steely blue eyes. "Progress? You call going into another trance in the middle of class 'progress'? We're right back where we started."

"She's had a minor setback. That's all. And I've already explained to you and Sister Mary Grace what happened."

"I know," he said, his voice weary. "But Summer can't keep tuning the world out every time she gets upset about something."

"She won't," Amanda assured him. "Try to understand. A confrontation with a teacher can be traumatic for any seven-year-old, but given one with Summer's background... Meditating was her way of dealing with the situation."

At his silence, Amanda pressed on. "Give it a little more time. Let me work with her—at least until the end of the school term. Two more months, that's all I'm asking for. That isn't very long."

"It is to me."

His eyes caught hers and held. Amanda saw clearly how much frustration their relationship and the restraints she'd placed on it had caused him. Had caused them both, she admitted.

In two short months Michael Grayson had managed to confuse her, tempt her, and make her question her resolve not to become involved with him. The fact that she'd agreed to meet him this evening after the rest of the staff had gone instead of waiting until the next day was only proof of just how involved she had become.

Knowing that she had broken her own rule and allowed their innocent conferences to become something more only added to her dismay.

"No, Amanda. I don't see any point in putting Summer...or *us* through any more of these sessions." He shoved his thick black hair away from his eyes. It fell stubbornly across his brow once again. "It's just not worth it."

The words were hard-edged—like the man himself, Amanda thought, studying the strong lines of his face, the firm set of his jaw.

She tried again. "What about Summer? Have you thought about how this is going to affect her?"

"Of course I have," he said, his voice gruff. "She's always been my first concern."

It was true, Amanda acknowledged silently. His devotion to his niece had been one of the things that had attracted her to him.

"Believe me, if the therapy was working, I'd stick with it regardless of how I felt about you. But it isn't. And seeing you, being with you week after week, trying to keep things between us on a professional level has been hell. I'm used to going after what I want, Amanda." His gaze slid from her eyes to her lips. "And I want you."

"Michael, don't."

"Don't what? Tell you that even when I'm not with you, I think about you? The way you look. The way you smell."

Amanda closed her eyes a moment and tried to slow the thudding of her heart.

"It's true. And I'm tired of you making excuses to keep me at arm's length."

"I'm not making excuses. I'm your niece's doctor."

Michael placed his hands flat on her desk and leaned forward, crowding her, filling her entire line of vision. "You're also a woman. There's no reason for us not to see each other if we want to."

"Michael, please. I've already explained. It would be unethical for us to . . . to become involved."

"You think we're not already involved?" he asked, his voice incredulous. "Are you going to deny that there's something between us? That you haven't felt this . . . this chemistry growing between us, pulling us together?"

Unable to deny his accusations, Amanda remained silent. It was true. She was attracted to him, had been from the moment she'd glimpsed the kind, caring man hidden behind the rough-edged persona he presented to the world. It was the gentle Michael who had somehow managed to sneak beneath her defenses.

"I've got news for you, sweetheart. Whether you admit it or not, we're involved. And as for those ethics you're so worried about, it's not a problem anymore. Because as of right now, you're no longer Summer's doctor."

Amanda swallowed. Perhaps it was best this way. If she would no longer be working with Summer, she would no longer be forced to see Michael. And if she didn't see him, talk to him, maybe these . . . these feelings he had awakened in her would wane.

Striving for some emotional distance, she tried to make her voice cool. "Very well, then. But if you change your mind and decide you want Summer to see another psychologist, there are several I can recommend." She reached for her Rolodex file.

Michael caught her wrist. "Dammit, Amanda. Haven't you heard anything I've said? I'm not interested in another psychologist."

Amanda stared into his stormy eyes and tried to ignore the effect of his nearness.

"What happened with Summer today is only part of the reason I'm calling the therapy quits. The other reason is us. I want there to be an 'us.'

"I'm through playing games. Either we see each other as two consenting adults, or we don't see each other at all." Releasing her wrist, he cupped her chin, forcing her to look at him. "What's it going to be? Yes or no?"

The word no stuck in her throat, lingered on the tip of her tongue.

She couldn't say it.

She *did* want to see Michael, to be with him. She'd been drawn to him from the start, had been surprised by the strength of that initial attraction. Even now, she couldn't explain it. Since her disastrous marriage to Adam, few men had been able to make her pulse race.

Michael Grayson had.

And somewhere along the way those innocent coffees they had shared after her sessions with Summer had turned into something more . . . something that both frightened and excited her at the same time. Somewhere along the way, she had grown to care for him.

She looked at his handsome face and silently chastised herself. How had she ever believed she could work with him, be with him, and keep her emotional distance? Hadn't she already proved she was a sucker for his type—a man who came as part of a package deal?

"Well, Amanda?" Michael's eyes searched hers.

She couldn't risk another mistake. The last one had cost her far too much. "I'm sorry, Michael. I can't."

An odd expression—something that resembled panic—crossed his face; but it disappeared so quickly, Amanda wondered if she'd imagined it.

His jaw hardened. Slowly he pulled back. Walking over to the chair, he picked up his sport coat, hooked it on his finger and slung it across one shoulder.

"Funny, I never pegged you for a coward. Despite all that blue blood and those oh-so-perfect manners, I thought you were a pretty gutsy lady. Guess you're not quite the woman I thought you were. My mistake." He started toward the door.

Suddenly she felt confused, unsure of herself. A sinking sensation washed over her at the prospect of him walking out of her life. "Michael, wait!"

He paused at the door and looked back at her.

"I—" She swallowed past the lump in her throat.

His expression wary, Michael retraced his steps across the room. He tossed his jacket on the chair and folded his arms across his chest. And waited.

Nervous, Amanda smoothed the skirt of her suit. Squaring her shoulders, she used all the poise she'd acquired as a diplomat's daughter to meet his gaze. "You're right," she said, trying to keep her voice even. "I've been using professional ethics as an excuse when my reasons are personal."

His expression softened. "Whatever it is, we can work it out. Just talk to me. Tell me what it is you're afraid of."

He made it sound so simple, but it wasn't. There were too many risks. Amanda shook her head. "There's really no point." Releasing a sigh, she continued. "Try to understand. I never meant for anything to happen between us. I don't want to become any more involved with you than I already am. I know from past experience that it...that we won't work."

Myriad emotions crossed Michael's face. "You know, you're not the only one with personal demons, Amanda. Maybe I'm letting some of my own demons cause me to overreact just as you have."

He sat down on the edge of her desk and toyed with the sleek silver pen that lay beside her appointment book. "Maybe you're right, maybe pulling Summer out of therapy now isn't the right thing to do." His gaze tangled with hers.

"Then you'll let her stay in the program?"

"I'm willing to discuss the possibility." He set down the pen. "But later. Right now, I have to get home. I left Summer with a sitter. I didn't want her sitting in the hall while you and I discussed her."

Amanda wasn't sure if she was relieved or disappointed. While her head told her to get him out of her life, her heart told her another story. Hooking a length of her hair behind one ear, she opened her appointment book. "When did you want to meet?"

"Friday."

She flipped the page and frowned. "It'll take some rescheduling, but I could see you at—"

"Seven o'clock. Over dinner."

Amanda looked up. "I don't think that's a good idea."

"I thought you wanted a chance to convince me to let Summer stay in the program?"

"I do."

"Then convince me on Friday." He shot her a slow, sexy smile that Amanda knew was meant to ease the tension, but didn't. "Come on. It's only dinner."

He was right. It was only dinner, she told herself. How much harm could there be in having dinner? "All right. Where should I meet you?"

"I'll pick you up."

"Michael, I don't think—"

"Try not to think so much," he said, leaning forward. "Sometimes it's better to just let yourself feel."

Gently he brushed his lips against hers. The contact was light, tender, a nonthreatening kiss. Yet the feel of his mouth, warm and firm against her own, sparked a fire inside her that seeped to her core.

Stifling the urge to pull her into his arms, Michael lifted his head. He looked into her brown eyes, all soft and dreamy, and checked the need to taste her lips again.

Slowly her dazed expression began to fade. "About Friday," she whispered.

He caught the note of doubt in her voice and refused to give her a chance to change her mind. "I'll pick you up at seven. Wear something casual.'' Easing off the desk, he retrieved his jacket and slipped out the door.

Standing outside the office, Michael drew a steadying breath. For a moment he'd been sure he'd blown it. He hadn't meant to issue her an ultimatum; and he certainly hadn't meant to kiss her. But the sight of that pretty pink mouth telling him no again, shooting holes in all his plans, had been too much.

As he headed for the exit, his thoughts were filled with Amanda. A slow burning began in the lower part of his body as he recalled the warmth of her lips, the sweet hesitation of her response.

He stepped out into the waning sunlight and started for the parking lot. He'd enjoyed that kiss—a lot more than he had bargained for. And for a few crazy moments he'd been tempted to shelve his plans.

He couldn't. Too much was at stake.

Frowning, Michael slipped inside the black sedan and removed the letter from his coat pocket. As he scanned the legal jargon once more, he thought back to that day six weeks ago when he'd decided to take his attorney's advice.

Find yourself a wife, Dave had said. *Summer needs a mother. You always said you were going to get married someday. Why not do it now?*

It had made perfect, logical sense. By taking a wife, he could give Summer the one thing she wanted most and the one thing Martha Winthrop with all her money and influence couldn't buy—a family. And what court would remove a child from a loving, two-parent home and opt for one with only a rich, elderly widow?

None, he'd told himself.

All he had to do was find a wife. The plan was simple. At least, he had thought so, until Summer had quickly dismissed each potential candidate he'd brought before her.

The only exception had been Amanda. She had been the only woman Summer seemed to truly like.

Shoving the letter back into his coat pocket, Michael started the engine and backed out of the parking lot.

Amanda was perfect. Not only was she beautiful, smart and interesting to be with, but she genuinely cared for his niece.

And she was attracted to him.

The feeling was mutual, he admitted. Moving the car into the line of traffic, he laughed out loud, the sound echoing inside the empty car. Who was he kidding? He'd been attracted to Amanda from the beginning. Over the past two months those feelings had only grown stronger…and they'd had nothing at all to do with Summer.

He wanted Amanda, period.

Michael's lips curved into a self-mocking smile. What red-blooded male wouldn't want her? With her pale blond hair and creamy skin, that long, sleek body, she looked more like a princess than a psychologist.

Granted, he was no prince. But he'd come a long way from the sixteen-year-old punk who'd lived on the wrong side of the tracks. Twenty years and a successful business could change a lot of things.

But it can't change who you are or who you have been, a small voice inside him whispered. Switching to the left lane, Michael frowned. He and his sister had both learned that no amount of money or success could make up for lack of the proper bloodlines. If he'd ever doubted it, the Winthrops had driven that point home when Sara had gotten pregnant.

Michael's fingers tightened on the steering wheel as all the bitter memories came back. He would protect Summer from them no matter what the cost—even if it meant using Amanda.

Guilt pricked at his conscience as he remembered the sad look in Amanda's velvety brown eyes.

He shoved it aside. He had no choice. He had to make Amanda fall in love with him and convince her to marry him.

And he had to do it soon because time was running out.

Amanda glanced around the cozy little restaurant, noting the candlelight, the soft music. The place Michael had chosen was charming, intimate, and threatened to sweep her resistance away. She would have preferred bright lights and noisy chatter. Absently, she traced the red-and-white squares of the tablecloth with her fingertip while Michael ordered a bottle of wine.

"I hope you like Italian food," he said.

She looked up and Michael flashed her a sexy grin that made her mouth dry. Tearing her gaze from his lips, she took a sip of water. "It's one of my favorites."

"Good. I thought about taking you to one of the more popular places in the Quarter, but I figured you'd probably been to most of them already and I wanted to take you someplace different."

Chiding herself for being so susceptible to him, Amanda was grateful when the waiter arrived with the wine. Anxious to put things back on a business footing, she said, "I hope you've given some more consideration to allowing Summer to continue with the counseling program."

"I have. Summer thinks quite a lot of you." He took a slow sip of his wine. "So do I," he said softly.

Heart pounding, Amanda reached for her wineglass.

As though sensing her uneasiness, Michael leaned back in his seat. He gave her a considering look. "You know, I've been curious. What made you decide to become a psychologist?"

Relieved by the change in subject, Amanda released her pent-up breath and tried to relax. "I guess you've probably heard that my father's an ambassador?"

Michael nodded.

"Well, as an ambassador's daughter, I got to attend a lot of receptions, ribbon cuttings, that sort of thing. Pretty boring stuff for a child." Amanda smiled weakly, remembering how lonely she had been. "And because of my father's position, it was important that I not do or say the wrong thing."

"Did you? Ever say or do something you shouldn't have?" Michael asked.

"Not unless you count the time I asked one of the Arab emirs why he needed three wives. Of course, I was only seven at the time," Amanda said, grinning.

Michael laughed, the sound rich and full of life. Then slowly the smile slipped from his lips. His deep blue eyes moved over her face like a caress. "I bet you were a beauty even then."

"Hardly. I had skinny legs and two missing front teeth," she quipped, unnerved by the sudden tension. "Anyway, I became good at studying people. When it was time for me to go to college, I decided to major in psychology. Gracie—Sister Mary Grace," she amended, "was one of my teachers. Since I liked working with kids, she encouraged me to specialize in child psychology."

Michael reached for her hand and squeezed it. "I, for one, am glad you followed her advice."

Warmed by his approval, Amanda studied him under the soft light. His hair, a dark, rich ebony, fell at an angle across his forehead and brushed the back collar of his shirt. Struck by the urge to smooth it with her fingertips, she shifted her gaze to his face.

At the look in his eyes, her pulse quickened. It had been a long time since any man had looked at her with such desire. And even longer, she admitted, since she had felt any response.

Shaken, Amanda pulled her hand free as the waiter served their salads.

"Since you like kids so much, I'm surprised you don't have any of your own."

Amanda's chest tightened. She had wanted children, had been thrilled to gain a stepdaughter when she'd married Adam. She had even hoped to fill their home with more children. But that had been before she'd discovered Adam's secret, before she'd suffered the humiliation of his deception. "Things don't always work out the way we plan," she said, trying to sound nonchalant.

"No, they don't." An odd expression crossed his face, then quickly disappeared. "Do you see much of your ex-husband's daughter since the divorce?"

"Kimberly and I—" Amanda paused, her fork in midair. "How did you know I had a stepdaughter?"

"Sister Mary Grace mentioned it."

Surprised, Amanda set down her fork. She narrowed her eyes. "Why on earth would she do that?"

Michael shrugged. "I was asking her about you and I guess it sort of came up in the conversation."

"I see," Amanda said, growing irritated. Dear friend or not, she wished she could get her hands around Gracie's neck.

"Don't be upset with Sister. I was the one asking the questions."

"Did it ever occur to you to ask me?"

"I did," he said, a slight edge in his voice. "But if you'll recall, you weren't exactly forthcoming."

"So you decided to ask Sister Mary Grace?"

"Yes," he replied evenly. "I told you, I believe in going after what I want."

And he wanted her, Amanda finished silently. "What else did the dear Sister tell you?" she asked, too annoyed by the thought of him learning the details of her personal life to keep the sarcasm from her voice.

"That you've been divorced about eighteen months, are disgusted with men in general, and that if my interest in you is genuine, I should be prepared for a tough battle." Michael flashed her a disarming grin. "She also said it was going to take a lot more than a handsome face and sexy smile to break through that Boston reserve of yours."

Amanda wanted to crawl under the table. "I can't believe she said that. She's a nun for heaven's sake."

"Yeah. Surprised me, too. I think she was trying to scare me off." Michael chuckled and shot her a considering look. "But as you can see, I don't frighten easily."

"Obviously," Amanda said, feeling exposed and vulnerable, and hating it.

"All I wanted was to get to know you better," he said gently. "I never meant to upset you."

"I'm not upset, just embarrassed." His sincerity touched her.

"There's no need to be." He gave her a disarming smile. "What do you say we call a truce and enjoy dinner? I promise Antonio's manicotti is the best in the city."

Amanda nodded her acquiesence.

Three hours later she was glad she had agreed to the truce. She couldn't remember the last time she had laughed so much in one evening—or had so much fun. And playing putt-putt, no less.

Smiling, Amanda leaned her head back against the seat of the car and listened to the soft melody playing on the radio as they headed for her home.

"Penny for your thoughts," Michael offered.

She shifted her gaze to him. "Only a penny?" she teased, feeling lighthearted. "The way you were trying to get me to bet on the outcome of that last game, I would have thought you were a much bigger gambler."

Michael chuckled. The sound was warm, intimate, inside the confines of the car. "How about a quarter, then?"

Amanda laughed. "Now that's what I call a big spender."

Exiting the interstate, Michael pulled the car to a stop at the red light. He turned to Amanda. The smile disappeared from his lips as he reached over and traced his thumb along the line of her jaw. "What's really going on inside that pretty head of yours?"

"I was thinking about what a nice time I had." Amanda swallowed, acutely aware of how close he was. In the darkness of the car, with only the dim light of the street lamp, his eyes reminded her of polished gems.

"Glad you came?"

"Yes," Amanda whispered. "I am."

"Me, too." He moved his thumb across her lower lip.

Amanda's heart pounded as he leaned closer. Frightened, excited, she closed her eyes and lifted her mouth.

A horn sounded behind them and Amanda pulled back.

Muttering, Michael yanked the gear shift, sending the car jerking forward. "Sorry," he mumbled as they sped down the dark street.

While he maneuvered the car through the city, Amanda studied the strong line of his jaw, the fullness of his mouth. Feelings, long buried, stirred to life inside her. She recalled how those lips had felt—warm and hungry against her own.

Realizing where her thoughts had drifted, she turned to stare out the window.

A few minutes later Michael pulled the car to a stop in front of her cottage and shut off the engine.

"Amanda?"

Pulling her gaze from the pink-and-white azaleas that lined the walkway to her home, she looked up. Michael stood in front of her, holding the door open.

Michael held her hand as she stepped out onto the driveway.

After closing the door, he pressed his hand to the small of her back and steered her toward the house.

It was a simple gesture of courtesy. Yet his touch made her nervous, edgy, acutely aware that she was a woman and he was a man. When they stepped into the alcove of her doorway, she wanted to race inside and bolt the door against him and the things he was making her feel.

"I had a great time tonight." He brushed a strand of hair away from her mouth. His fingertips caressed her cheek. "When can I see you again?"

He was so close, she could see the faint shadow along his jaw that would demand a razor's edge in the morning. The night seemed to close in around her. The sweet scent of gardenias faded and was replaced with the scent of woods, of earth. Of Michael.

Michael sucked in his breath. "Amanda, don't look at me like that."

She looked up and saw her own hunger mirrored in his eyes. "Like what?"

"Like you want me," he said in a voice husky with desire. Extending his arms on either side of her head, he placed his palms flat against the door, trapping her within his embrace. "Like you want to touch me. Taste me." His gaze fell to her mouth. "The way I want to touch and taste you."

Knees weak, Amanda leaned back, grateful for the solid door. As Michael lowered his head, she braced her hands against his chest, intent on pushing him away.

She leaned toward him instead.

And then his mouth touched hers.

His kiss was just as she remembered it. Gentle, coaxing, a slow brushing of lips against lips. He took her bottom lip into his mouth and nibbled, slowly explored its shape with his tongue.

Unable to stop herself, Amanda touched the tip of her tongue to his.

Michael shuddered. His heart beat like a drum against her fingertips and she strained closer. When his tongue began another slow foray of her mouth, Amanda's control broke. She curled her fingers into his shirt, crumpling the soft cotton in her fists.

When Amanda's tongue darted into his mouth, Michael thought he would explode. This time there was no hesitancy. This time there was fire; this time there was passion.

He crushed her to him, tangled his fingers in her silky hair.

A whimper escaped her lips, making his body burn anew. Not since he'd been a teenager had he responded so wildly to a kiss. Not since he'd been a young man had he wanted something so much. Never in his life had that something been a woman.

Until now.

This doesn't mean anything, Amanda told herself as she leaned against him. It was simply a matter of chemistry... of proximity.

It was more than that. And she knew it. Suddenly frightened by the realization, Amanda pushed at his chest.

Easing his hold, Michael drew away slightly. He looked into her eyes, smoky and warm with desire.

"Michael."

"Shh." He dropped another kiss on her lips. The sight of Amanda's beautiful face flushed, her mouth swollen from his kisses, caused his body to ache even more. He pulled her back into his arms.

"No," she whispered, panic seizing her. Kissing Michael had been insanity on her part. "This was a mistake."

"It wasn't a mistake," he insisted, hearing the alarm in her voice and not understanding it. He stroked her hair, wanting to reassure her.

Amanda heard the denial in his voice, saw the yearning in his eyes. She stepped back, out of his arms. Taking a deep breath, she filled her lungs with fresh air, trying to clear her senses. How could she have done this? Let things get so out of hand?

"Don't push me away, Amanda."

"Please, Michael. It was just a kiss," she said, deliberately sounding flip. "Let's not make it into more than it was."

Michael stiffened. Just a kiss? He dropped his hands to his sides. It was a hell of a lot more than a simple kiss and they both knew it.

"Thank you for dinner," she continued primly as though nothing had happened. But Michael heard the slight catch in her voice, saw the tremor of her lips.

"We'll have to do it again—soon." He edged a little closer and experienced a small measure of satisfaction at the flash of panic that clouded her brown eyes.

Just as quickly, she schooled her expression and retrieved her keys from her purse.

Michael took them from her fingers. Unlocking the door, he pushed it open.

"Well, thanks again," she murmured politely.

"Aren't you going to ask me in for a nightcap?" he baited, irritated with her for denying there was something between them and with himself for caring.

Amanda shot him a look that would, no doubt, quell a lesser man. "No, I'm not," she said in those crisp, clear tones that had made him peg her as a New Englander the first time he'd met her.

Michael bit down on his anger at her rejection. "Then next time," he managed.

"There won't be any next time," she said, tipping up her chin.

The haughtiness of her tone caused something to snap inside him. Before he could stop himself, Michael reached for her. Cupping the back of her head, he pulled her to him. "I promise you there will be a next time, Amanda. Tonight was only the beginning."

Three

Amanda glanced at the small, crystal clock sitting on her desk. Four-twenty. The knot in her stomach tightened. Only ten more minutes before Michael arrived.

Unable to concentrate, she closed the file folder she had been studying and, walking across the room, she gazed out the window to the school playground at the dozen or so children who had remained for after-school care.

Hearing a squeal of laughter, Amanda smiled as she spotted Summer—her long, dark braids flying behind her while she raced across the yard engaged in a game of tag.

She wasn't at all the same child she had been when they had started working together ten weeks ago, Amanda thought. Sad and withdrawn, it had been so heartening to gain the little girl's trust, to help her sort through her confusion and pain at her mother's death. Of course, Michael's love and attention had made her job easier by far.

Michael.

Amanda cursed herself for thinking of him again. It was pointless to think about him.

Instead she focused on Summer's smiling face, and her heartstrings tugged once more. She was going to miss the child. But there was nothing she could do. And considering the outcome of her last encounter with Michael, perhaps it was for the best. She certainly couldn't risk another evening like the previous Friday's.

Amanda touched her lips, recalling all too vividly how that evening had ended. Longing, hot and demanding, flickered through her as she remembered the feel of Michael's lips, the warmth of his breath, the hardness of his body against her own. Squeezing her eyes shut, she fought back a groan as she recalled her own wanton response.

"Amanda?"

She tensed at the sound of Michael's voice. She wasn't ready to face him—not yet, not when the memory of his kiss was so fresh.

"The secretary *did* say four-thirty, didn't she?"

Attempting to school her expression, Amanda turned around slowly. "Yes. Please, come in."

When he closed the door and stepped inside, the room seemed somehow smaller. "You can sit down, if you'd like." She gestured toward the chair across from her desk.

He cut across the room in swift, easy strides, stopping in front of her. "I tried to reach you all weekend," he said softly, his eyes searching hers.

"I know. I got your messages." All *five* messages. And because the temptation to pick up the telephone and talk to him had been so strong, she had deliberately spent her weekend working in the garden and stalking the city's shopping centers. She'd tried on clothes she neither needed nor wanted only to return home empty-handed and exhausted. When the calls had persisted, she had taken herself off to a movie.

"Why didn't you return my calls?"

Amanda met his questioning gaze. "I thought it best not to."

"Better for whom?" he asked, frowning.

"For me. And possibly for you, too."

"You're wrong," he said, a slight edge in his voice. "On both counts. There's something good between us, Amanda, and you know it. What are you so afraid of?"

You, she wanted to shout. The things you make me feel, the things you make me want. The risks you make me want to take.

Instead she simply said, "I told you before, my reasons for not going out with you are personal. I have no desire to explain those reasons to you and I doubt that you'd understand them even if I did. The problem is me, Michael—not you. But, believe me, I'm serious when I tell you you're wasting your time. There can't ever be anything between us."

"What about last Friday?" he demanded. "Are you going to tell me it didn't mean anything to you? That it was nothing?"

"Last Friday was very special." For a few short hours she had been able to put the past and its painful scars behind her. But despite the explosive chemistry and her growing feelings for him, Michael was still a man with a child—a child very much in need of a mother. She wouldn't take a chance on being used again.

"I had a lovely time, but it was still a mistake. A relationship with you would mean too many complications and I don't want or need any more complications in my life. Please accept that."

"I can't." His jaw clenched; a muscle ticked angrily in his cheek. "And I'm not going to let you accept it, either. I won't let you throw us away, Amanda."

Amanda tipped up her chin. "You don't have a choice. I have no intention of going out with you again and now that Summer's no longer in therapy, there's no reason for us to see each other at all."

"But that's where you're wrong." His lips smoothed into a slow, knowing smile. "We *will* be seeing each other. You see, I'm giving you the two months with Summer that you asked for. I'm not taking her out of your program. In fact, I've already told her she can stay. So, you and I will be seeing each other—a lot—at least for the next couple of months.''

"But I thought…'' Surprised and unsettled by his change in attitude, Amanda turned away. "When Summer didn't show up for her appointment yesterday, I assumed you'd withdrawn her from the program.''

"Then you assumed wrong.''

She had been so sure she wouldn't have to see him again after today. Now she would be faced with not only seeing him but with dealing with the memories and desires he sparked in her.

"Don't you remember me telling you last week that Summer had a dental appointment and wouldn't be able to come on Monday?''

Vaguely, Amanda recalled the words, but at the time she'd been so disturbed by the way he'd been looking at her that she had failed to write it down.

"Did you really think I'd just pull her out of the program without telling you first? Especially after you tried so hard to convince me to let her stay?'' His voice held a wealth of disappointment.

That was exactly what she had thought. And it had made her decision not to see him again easier somehow.

"You don't have to bother answering that. It's obvious what you thought.'' He took a deep breath and released it. "For the record, you were right. Summer does need help. Help that I can't give her. I was a fool to even consider pulling her out of the program. She needs you, Amanda. *I* need you. Will you help me?''

She wanted to refuse him.

She couldn't, not when he was looking at her with such warmth in his eyes.

"All right,'' Amanda answered, her voice thick. "I'll keep working with Summer until the end of the school term—but on one condition. We keep our relationship strictly professional. Agreed?''

When he didn't respond, Amanda gave him a stern look that she usually reserved for the children. "I want your promise, Michael.''

He shook his head. "I'm afraid I can't give it to you. If I did, I'd only end up breaking it. And I make it a point never to go back on my word."

Feeling trapped, Amanda walked back to the window and stared out at the playground. She was committed to Summer and didn't want to abandon her now. She felt a responsibility to the little girl. But what about herself? Was she strong enough to resist the emotional threat Michael represented?

She sensed him come up behind her, her body suddenly alert at his nearness.

"Amanda?" He touched her shoulder and turned her to face him.

He was so close, she could smell the woodsy scent of his cologne, see the sprinkling of gray at his temples.

"Why are you doing this to us?" His eyes held hers. "Is it because of the things you've heard about me? About my family?"

Amanda flushed. "Of course not."

"Then why won't you even give us a chance?"

"Amanda?" A quick, one-two tap followed at the door. "Do you still have the fi—" Sister Mary Grace stopped and stared from the doorway. She looked from Amanda to Michael and back again. "Excuse me," she said, and started to retreat from the room.

"Gra—Sister, wait." Quickly, Amanda pulled away and moved past Michael. Embarrassed, she could have cringed at the sight they must have made. What must Gracie be thinking after practically catching her in Michael's arms? "Did you want to see me about something?" she asked, trying to muster as much dignity as she could under the circumstances.

"Nothing that can't wait until later. I didn't realize you had someone with you." Turning toward Michael, she said, "Forgive me for interrupting. You two go ahead and finish your, um, discussion. I can speak to Amanda later."

"No!" Amanda cried out as Sister Mary Grace started to leave. She swallowed and then continued more calmly, "Mr. Grayson and I are finished. He was just leaving."

Sister Mary Grace arched one brow; the look she gave
Amanda left her with little doubt that the nun didn't believe her.

"It's okay, Sister." Michael moved toward the door.
"Amanda's right. We are finished—for now."

Amanda caught the warning in his voice, but refused to
meet his gaze.

"Sister." He inclined his head toward the nun, then
turned to Amanda. "I'll see you tomorrow."

"Tomorrow?" Amanda repeated, and could have kicked
herself at the anxious sound of her voice.

"After Summer's appointment," he informed her. "She
is still scheduled for Wednesday, isn't she?"

"Yes. Yes, of course."

"See you then."

Once Michael had closed the door, Amanda breathed a
sigh of relief. Returning to her desk, she sat down and directed her attention back to her friend. "Now, what was it
you needed?" she asked, forcing a lightness she didn't feel.

"What was *that* all about?" Sister Mary Grace asked as
she claimed the chair in front of Amanda's desk.

Ignorning the bright gleam in her friend's eyes, Amanda
returned evenly, "Michael came by to tell me he's decided
to allow Summer to remain in the therapy program."

"Why, that's excellent news. I mean, I know he was having some doubts about the program's effectiveness. I'm glad
to see you were able to bring him around."

Sister Mary Grace adjusted the wire-rimmed spectacles on
her nose, then met Amanda's eyes. "But something tells me
his niece isn't the only reason Michael Grayson came to see
you."

Amanda shot her friend a stony look.

The tiny nun grinned. "Come on, Mandy. The man
hasn't exactly made his interest in you a secret. And I kind
of got the impression that you liked him, too."

"Gracie." Amanda made no attempt to hide her dis-
pleasure.

"I know, I know. I shouldn't interfere, but you're my
friend. I'm only trying to help."

"How? By encouraging him? Telling him personal things about me? How could you do that?"

Sister Mary Grace's smile faded. Her rosy cheeks paled slightly. "I didn't mean any harm."

At the nun's stricken expression, Amanda immediately regretted her flare of temper. "I know you didn't, and I'm sorry for biting your head off. But don't you see? Encouraging him was the worst thing you could do."

"Why? What's wrong with a nice, young man showing an interest in you?"

"Everything—if that man's Michael Grayson. You of all people should know I could never become involved with a man like him."

Sister Mary Grace frowned. "What do you mean, 'a man like him'? From everything I've seen, and from what you've told me yourself, he's a fine, honorable man."

"He is. But for someone else. Not me."

"Any why not you?" Sister Grace asked in that impervious tone that Amanda had always found so frustrating.

"Because he has a child."

Sister Mary Grace narrowed her eyes. She folded her arms across her chest. "As far as I know, Michael Grayson doesn't have any children," she said in that no-nonsense voice of hers. "In fact, according to the information he gave the school when he registered Summer, he's never even been married."

"Quit fencing, Gracie. You know perfectly well what I mean. He has Summer."

"So? She's his niece."

"Yes, but for all intents and purposes, she's his child. He's the one raising her."

"And doing a fine job of it, too. So, what's the problem?"

Frustrated, Amanda glared at her friend. "You know what the problem is. He has a seven-year-old child who needs a mother. You saw what happened in Mrs. Green's class last week when they started talking about the Mother's Day project. The poor thing was completely distraught."

"Yes, I saw. And I also saw how much you care about that little girl. That was a wonderful thing you did, agreeing to go to the Mother Daughter Luncheon with her next month."

"Perhaps I shouldn't have." It had been a foolish thing to do, given her own history. But then, it had broken her heart to see Summer so despondent.

Sister Mary Grace patted her hand. "Of course, you should have."

"I've been down this road before, Gracie. I know where it leads and all the traps it can hold. I don't want to be used again. And I'm not going to put myself in a position where I can be used again—by Michael Grayson or anyone else."

Sister Mary Grace rose. She came around the desk and put her arms around Amanda's shoulders. "Mandy, Mandy," she soothed. "When are you going to stop punishing yourself for someone else's mistakes?"

"I'm not. I'm protecting myself."

"That's a lot of malarkey and you know it. You don't give yourself or anyone else a chance. You set up obstacles the minute any man shows an interest in you."

"That's not true."

Sister Mary Grace pulled back and looked at Amanda. "Isn't it?"

Was Gracie right? Was she setting up obstacles? True, Summer did chatter endlessly about getting a new mother someday; but the little girl spoke almost just as often about finding some imaginary grandmother, as well.

On the other hand, Michael had been decidedly quiet on both subjects—even when she had expressed her concern about Summer's preoccupation with them. In fact, Michael had given no indication that he even *thought* he needed a wife—let alone was looking for one.

But then, neither had Adam—at least not until after he had courted her, had played to her foolish dreams, had made her believe he loved her, made her fall in love with him. And when it had been too late, when she had married him and moved into his home, she had found out the truth.

Sister Mary Grace's expression softened. "Hasn't it ever occurred to you that Michael's interest in you could be motivated by nothing more than the simple fact that he likes you? You're a lovely woman, Amanda. Isn't it just possible, he finds you attractive?"

Remembering the heat in his eyes, the hunger of his kiss, Amanda didn't doubt that Michael found her attractive. She thought of the way his body had hardened at her response. Not even Adam, master actor that he was, had made her feel so desired, so much like a woman. But then, she had been naive and trusting.

She wasn't anymore.

"Why not give him the benefit of the doubt? What have you got to lose?"

Everything. Her heart, what was left of her pride. "I can't, Gracie. There are too many risks involved. And I'm through taking risks."

"Not even for love?"

"Especially not for love. The price is too high." And one she was unwilling to pay.

Propping the telephone between his shoulder and ear, Michael kicked the door to his bedroom shut and listened to the worried voice of his attorney, Dave Jennings.

"Come on, Mike, be reasonable. Let me set up a meeting with old lady Winthrop and her attorney and try to work something out."

"There's nothing to work out. I told you, Martha Winthrop gave up any rights she might have had when that son of hers turned his back on my sister. If it hadn't been for her, Sara never would have run away in the first place. She wouldn't have been on that damn mountain, wouldn't have..." His voice broke; he choked back the pain thoughts of his sister's death caused and hardened his resolve. "I'll *never* give that woman access to Summer."

Dave's sigh came through loud and weary over the phone line. "All right. We'll play it your way. But I sure hope you know what you're doing because I wasn't kidding about the sympathy factor being in Martha Winthop's favor. Things have changed a lot in the last few years. The courts are ruling in favor of the grandparents in quite a number of these cases involving grandparents' rights—even ones where illegitimacy is a factor. If Martha Winthrop sues you for custody of Summer, there's a strong possibility that she'll win and you'll lose Summer.''

"I won't," he said determinedly. Michael's chest tightened painfully at the very thought of losing Summer. In the few short months since she'd come to live with him, the little girl had turned his entire life upside down and had stolen his heart in the process. Now he couldn't imagine himself without her.

"I hope you're right, pal . . . for everyone's sake."

"You know what your problem is, Dave? You worry too much," Michael informed him. "I'm not going to lose Summer. I told you, I've got a plan." He *wouldn't* lose Summer. He couldn't.

"So you've said." Michael caught the hint of skepticism in his friend's tone. "But since you haven't seen fit to tell me just what this brilliant plan of your is, don't blame me if I'm not quite as confident as you are that everything's going to be just fine."

How could he explain to his friend or anyone else that he was banking on marriage to Amanda swaying things in his favor? "It will be." It simply had to.

"Suit yourself. But whatever this foolproof plan of your is, it had better come together soon because I'm not going to be able to stall much longer. The only reason Martha Winthrop hasn't taken you to court already is because I indicated to her attorney you might come around. The woman's not stupid, Mike. I'm not going to be able to keep putting her off."

"You won't have to. All I need is a few more weeks." And a small miracle, Michael added silently as he hung up the phone.

After years of successfully avoiding the grand delusion of love and marriage that so many of his friends had succumbed to, he had finally decided to step into the trap; only the woman he'd chosen was proving to be less than willing.

Maybe because in his past relationships, the woman always knew and shared his need for pleasure without commitment. Despite the ritzy social circles and the privileged upbringing her family's position had obviously provided, there was something about Amanda that struck him as a little old-fashioned. His lips curved at the thought of an old-fashioned, morally conscious heart hidden beneath all that pale blond beauty and sophistication.

Opening his closet, he took out a white polo shirt and a pair of jeans, and changed his clothes. Somehow, he didn't think Amanda was the type of woman who would settle for an affair. She didn't strike him as one of the love-without-commitment breed.

The big thing he did have going for him was that she was attracted to him physically. He'd dispelled any doubts he'd had on that score the first time they'd kissed. Getting her to fall in love with him *should* have been easy. It had been anything but. Every time he'd made any headway, she would shy away like a skittish colt—the way she had today.

Remembering their earlier encounter, Michael thought about the way her eyes, that rich dark shade of coffee, had looked at him with such longing, how sweet her lips had tasted.

His jeans grew painfully tight and Michael frowned, disturbed by how just the thought of her made him ache. Even more disturbing was that it was becoming more difficult to remember that his seduction of Amanda was part of his plan to save Summer.

A flicker of guilt tugged at him again, but he pushed it aside. It wasn't as if he would be using her and giving nothing in return. Theirs would be a true marriage in every sense of the word.

The very thought of making love to Amanda, feeling, tasting all that beautiful soft skin, made his body burn even more.

Muttering a curse, Michael shoved his bare feet into a pair of Top-Siders. The woman was not only messing up his plan but she had him feeling like a teenager.

He didn't like the feeling.

Right now, he had to figure out a way to ease Amanda's fears, whatever they were; otherwise, there was little chance she would fall in love with and marry him.

Yanking open the bedroom door, Michael headed downstairs in search of Summer. "Hey, Shortstuff. Where are you?" he called out affectionately.

"In here, Uncle Mike."

Following the sound of her voice, Michael went into the den. Black-and-white saddle oxfords and a pair of white socks lay discarded next to the sofa. Still dressed in her pleated navy skirt and white blouse, Summer knelt in front of the wood-and-glass coffee table, her head bent over a stack of envelopes.

Michael walked across the carpet and tweaked one of her long, black braids. "What are you doing?"

She looked up at him out of those huge green eyes and smiled. "I'm addressing the invitations to my birthday party next week." She held up one for him to inspect.

"Nice." Stooping down beside her, he studied the bright red-and-yellow party invitation announcing the celebration of her eighth birthday at the Pizza Palace. He glanced over at the list written in her little girl script containing the names of her classmates. "Need any help?"

"Nope." She shook her head and reached for another envelope. "This is the last one except for..." Summer paused and turned to Michael. "I'm inviting Sister Mary Grace and Mrs. Green to the party. Do you think it would be okay to invite Dr. Bennett, too?"

"I don't see why not," Michael said, pleased by the idea.

"Do you think she'll come?"

"I'm sure she will if she can. Amanda likes you a lot."

Summer's face split into a big smile. "I like her a lot, too."

The following Friday, Amanda knew she had made a mistake in coming to Summer's birthday party. Despite the noise and chatter at the Pizza Palace, she was far too aware of Michael sitting directly across from her.

Unable to stop herself, she watched Michael's tongue flick tomato sauce from his bottom lip before he bit into the pizza.

It's lust, she told herself, ignoring the kick of emotion she had experienced when she'd walked in and seen him, looking sexy and appealing in charcoal jeans and an oxford shirt while he joked with the children.

She admired and respected him for trying to make Summer's first birthday without her mother a happy one, she told herself. Her feelings went no deeper than that. She wouldn't allow them to.

And as for her response to his kisses ... He was an attractive man and an excellent kisser, she reasoned. Her reaction had been that of any healthy female.

"What's the matter? Have I got cheese stuck on my chin?"

Amanda blinked. "I beg your pardon?"

Michael wiped his mouth with a napkin, then grinned. "You were staring. And I thought maybe I'd smeared pizza sauce on my face."

Amanda could feel the color rise to her cheeks. "No. No pizza sauce," she said, and reached for her mug of root beer.

"Don't you like your pizza, Dr. Bennett?" Summer asked.

Amanda's gaze swiveled to the child seated to Michael's left. "Why, yes. It's delicious."

"Then I guess pepperoni's just not your favorite."

"Pepperoni's fine." Amanda glanced down the table at the other children busily devouring the huge pans of pizza. She furrowed her brows. "Why would you think it wasn't?"

"Because you're still nibbling on your first slice," Michael answered as he reached for another piece.

"Guess I'm just a slow eater." Amanda picked up her half-eaten slice of pizza. She bit into the thick crust and tore off a chunk with her teeth, capturing the threads of gooey cheese with her tongue.

Summer reached for another slice. "I bet it would taste even better with anchovies."

Michael grimaced. "Not everybody has your cast-iron stomach, Shortstuff."

Amanda laughed and, for the first time in a long while, she relaxed.

When the pizza was finished and they moved to the seats in front of the puppet stage, she didn't object when Michael insisted she sit next to him.

And later, when the marionettes enthralled the children with their antics on the stage, she didn't pull away when Michael caught her hand, entwining her fingers with his own.

Cutting a glance to her right, she studied the hard line of his jaw, the deeply tanned skin exposed by the open neck of his shirt.

She'd heard the stories that had circulated among the teachers and school staff. He wasn't a man who let things or people stand in the way of what he wanted. "Ruthless" some had said. It was rumored that with little more than sheer determination, he'd wrestled the ownership of a small, troubled construction company from the grasp of a much bigger and wealthier competitor. And in record time, he'd turned the failing concern into one of the most successful businesses in the city.

Remembering the determined gleam in his eyes when he had told her that he went after what he wanted, Amanda could believe the stories were true. Her breath quickened.

And he wanted her.

Suddenly the sound of applause registered, breaking her reverie. Amanda shifted her attention to the stage just as the curtain came down. Releasing her hand, Michael clapped loudly, occasionlly piercing the air with one of those long shrill whistles that only men seemed to know how to do.

Once the applause subsided, one of the clowns employed by the Pizza Palace handed Michael a stack of small envelopes.

After thanking him, Michael turned to the chattering youngsters. "Okay, who wants to play video games?"

A chorus of "Me's" rang out as the children jumped up and down excitedly, holding out their small hands.

"Want to help?" he asked Amanda.

"Sure." She took half of the envelopes and began distributing one packet of tokens per child. When she'd finished, she held out the two remaining envelopes to Michael. "Looks like you have a few extras."

"Wrong. These are for us. Come on." He took her arm and led her toward the aisle of video and pinball machines where Summer and her friends were playing with great enthusiasm. The air hummed with a steady flow of electronic zips, zaps and pings, followed by a series of squeals or groans, depending on the success of the game.

"Looks like we don't have a lot of choices," Michael said leading her to the only open spot on the row—a pinball machine. Standing on four chrome legs, the flat surface base stretched out before them in an intricate maze of numbers and yellow bumper lights. A thin alley holding five fist-size chrome balls sat waiting at the base of the maze, a pull lever resting against the first one. The scoreboard towered above the game, the face of a wizard painted in bright slashes of red, yellow and green with black squares for eyes that still read the last challenger's score. Lights wreathed its borders.

"How are you against the Pinball Wizard?" Michael asked.

"I don't know. I've never played a pinball machine before," Amanda confessed. "For that matter, I've never played a video game, either."

"Never?" he asked, his disbelief obvious.

"Never."

Michael shook his head, but his eyes brightened with laughter. "You know, Dr. Bennett, despite those fancy schools you went to, I'm beginning to think your education has been sadly lacking in the subject of fun."

"Maybe you're right," she said, smiling.

"Well, we're going to have to see what we can do about that."

Amanda laughed. Maybe that explained her attraction to Michael, she thought. He made her nervous and he made her yearn for things she thought she no longer wanted, but he also made her laugh—something she hadn't done in a very long time.

"You're not supposed to laugh at the teacher." He shot her a stern look, but his eyes were filled with amusement. "I can see I've got my work cut out for me. Hand over one of your tokens."

Amanda did as he instructed.

He slipped the coin into the slot and the scoreboard lit up. "Come here." He motioned for her to stand in front of him.

He moved behind her, fencing her in when he extended his arms on either side of her to rest on the machine, his legs just brushing the backs of hers.

"Now, pay attention. I'm going to teach you the fine art of playing pinball."

Thirty minutes later the smile had slipped from her lips and Amanda found it impossible to concentrate. Down to her last token, Amanda prayed that she would lose the game—quickly.

"You're not concentrating, Amanda. Do it like this," Michael said, moving his body in behind hers. He slipped his arms around her as he attempted to show her how to line up the shot.

His hard chest pressed against her back; his legs brushed against her calves.

"Come on, try leaning into it." The warmth of his breath feathered her ear.

Heart pounding, Amanda fumbled with the levers and missed. "I give up. I'm no good at this."

"Sure you are. You just need more practice. Come on, let's play another game."

"No," Amanda said firmly, easing out of Michael's arms. She glanced at the wall clock and was stunned at how quickly the afternoon had passed. She'd only come because it had seemed to mean so much to Summer. She certainly hadn't planned to stay for the entire party. "I had no idea it was so late. I'd better be getting home."

Summer deserted the machine she'd been playing a few feet away and rushed over to her. "You can't go yet, Dr.

Bennett. Not until we cut my birthday cake. Please, say you'll stay until we cut the cake."

Amanda looked down into the small heart-shaped face, moved by the plea in the little girl's voice. She smoothed the bangs away from Summer's eyes. "Of course, I'll stay. Besides, I haven't given you my present yet."

"Can we cut the cake now, Uncle Mike?"

"Sure."

"Come on, everybody. It's time to cut the cake," Summer called out. She held out one of her hands to Amanda. Taking it, Amanda closed her fingers around the small, delicate fingers. Michael took Summer's other hand and the three of them walked over to the table already surrounded by excited seven- and eight-year-olds.

The pizza pans had been cleared away; the table had been trimmed in red and white. A huge cake bearing the image of the Little Mermaid rested in the center.

At Michael's request, Amanda lit the candles and after the children finished singing Happy Birthday, she stooped down next to Summer. "Ready to make a wish?"

Summer looked at her, the light flickering atop the cake reflecting in her green eyes. "Do all birthday wishes come true?" she asked.

"I'm not sure about all of them, but a lot of them do."

Summer gave her a shy grin. "I hope mine comes true." She squeezed her eyes shut a moment, then drew in a deep breath and released it.

As the children cheered, Amanda swallowed past a lump in her throat and wondered what Summer had wished for. Had she wished for the new mother she had been hoping her uncle would provide her with? Or for the mysterious grandmother she was so sure existed?

Amanda glanced over Summer's head at Michael. His blue eyes were fixed on her face, his expression serious; that determined gleam was back in his eyes. A wave of apprehension shuddered through Amanda.

Whatever his niece had wished for, Amanda was sure of one thing. Michael would move mountains to make sure that the little girl's wish came true.

Four

————

"Thank you for allowing Matthew to come to Summer's party, Mrs. Stuart."

"Oh, you're most welcome, Mr. Grayson. Matthew had a wonderful time. Didn't you, dear?"

Michael shook the young boy's hand. While he continued to murmur polite thank-yous to the parents collecting their children, Michael's gaze kept drifting to Amanda. She and Summer were seated at a table, chairs pulled close, their heads bent slightly, almost touching. Summer fingered the carousel music box Amanda had given her for her birthday while she listened intently to what Amanda was saying.

Carefully, Summer rewrapped the gift in its white tissue and returned it to the box on the table. Then, her green eyes glowing with happiness, she threw her arms around Amanda's neck.

Michael swallowed, experiencing a sharp kick somewhere in the region of his heart at the scene in front of him. Here was the motherly affection Summer had been longing for, that she'd cried for when she'd told him she missed her mother, the one need his own love could never give her.

Emotion churned inside him, making him feel frustrated, helpless. He angled his gaze back to Amanda.

A pained, almost yearning expression flickered across her features momentarily, then she closed her eyes and hugged Summer to her.

Not for the first time Michael wondered what had brought that shadowed look to her eyes. Was it her ex-husband? She'd said little about her failed marriage and had seemed reluctant to discuss it at all. Michael frowned. Had she loved the other man deeply and been hurt a great deal by the divorce? Was that the reason she was so cautious? So distrustful? Was it possible she still loved her ex-husband?

Michael scowled, something dark and unfamiliar unfurling inside him at the thought of Amanda with another man, as someone else's wife.

Whatever feelings she might still harbor for her ex-husband, he would wipe them away, Michael promised himself. She was going to be *his* wife. He didn't want anyone else.

Michael studied the lines of her delicately sculptured face, the generous pink mouth.

It had to be her. No one else would do.

She was going to be his.

It was time to stop pussyfooting around, he told himself. He needed to take advantage of whatever physical attraction she felt for him and turn it into something more. He'd never taken things slow and easy in his business dealings or in his relationships with women before. He shouldn't have done it this time, either.

As the last of her school friends approached to say their goodbyes to Summer, Amanda released her. Standing, Amanda smoothed the lines of her pale blue slacks and started in his direction.

Yes, Michael decided, he'd made a mistake in allowing Amanda to dictate the pace of their relationship. She spent far too much time thinking and analyzing. From now on, he was going to concentrate on making her feel.

His mouth eased into a grin. And he was going to thoroughly enjoy every minute of the process.

"Looks like the party was a big success," Amanda said, stopping in front of him. "I had a lovely time. Thank you for inviting me."

Her lips curved into a smile, yet he detected a sadness, a vulnerability that had been missing earlier. "Actually it was Summer's idea. But if she hadn't asked you to come, I would have," he said tenderly.

"Yes, well, thank you again." Averting her eyes, Amanda glanced in Summer's direction. "I guess I'd better let you get back to Summer and her guests."

Michael followed the direction of her gaze. Only Summer, her best friend and the little girl's mother remained. The three of them were busily boxing up the birthday gifts. "I think they can manage without me for a few minutes. Come on, I'll walk you to your car."

"Thanks, but it's really not necessary. I'm parked just outside in the lot."

"But I insist," he said, placing his hand at her back.

After asking Michelle's mother to keep an eye on Summer, Michael led Amanda outside. The afternoon sun peeked from behind a cloud, its rays turning her hair a pale shade of gold.

"This is my car," she said, stopping next to a silver BMW.

After unlocking the door, Michael placed the key in her hand and closed her fingers over the metal ring. When he didn't release her hand, Amanda looked up.

"I was afraid you might not come today," he said softly. "I'm glad you did."

She met his gaze squarely, but Michael didn't miss the caution flickering in those dark eyes. "Michael, I came because of Summer."

"I know." He moved a step closer.

"It seemed to mean a lot to her that I be here."

"It did. And it meant a lot to me, too." He released her hand and gently drew his finger down her cheek. Her skin was soft and smooth and reminded him of expensive silk. He stared at her mouth, remembering how sweet she had tasted. He leaned a fraction closer, wanting to taste that sweetness again.

"Michael." She said his name in a breathless way that sounded like part protest and part plea.

With effort, he checked the urge to pull her close. Now wasn't the time, he told himself. A public parking lot in broad daylight was not where he wanted to be when he kissed her again.

Dropping his hand to his side, he opened her car door. Amanda slid onto the seat.

Still holding the door handle with one hand, he braced his other hand along the edge of the car roof just over the driver's seat and leaned forward. His eyes sought hers. "Have dinner with me tonight?" he asked, not wanting to wait until next week to see her again.

"I can't."

"Tomorrow night, then?"

Amanda shook her head, her expression impossibly sad. "I'm sorry. I just can't." She started the engine.

Straightening, Michael closed her car door, then stood back, surprised by the strength of his disappointment. He had genuinely wanted to be with her, he admitted, and once more she had run away.

As he watched the small silver car disappear into traffic, a new restlessness stirred within him. They were going to be together, he vowed silently. She was going to be his. And soon.

Ignoring the voice deep inside him that questioned these new feelings of possessiveness Amanda aroused in him, Michael turned and strode back to the Pizza Palace.

Thirty minutes later Michael's thoughts were still filled with Amanda as he and Summer headed for home.

"What's the matter, Uncle Mike? Didn't you have a good time at my party?" Summer asked.

Michael cut a glance to his right. "Sure, pumpkin. I had a great time. What about you?"

Summer's mouth split into a wide grin. "It was the best birthday I ever had."

"I'm glad," he said, ruffling her hair.

"I only wish..." Her smile slipped a notch.

"What is it, honey? What were you wishing for?"

Summer shrugged. "I was just wishing my mom were still alive... that she could have been there to see all the stuff I got."

"I know, sweetheart. So do I." Michael's chest tightened at the thought of his sister. Sara *should* have been there for her daughter's birthday, and she would have been were it not for the Winthrops.

"But I'm glad Dr. Bennett came," Summer said, brightening a little. "She's very nice."

"Yes, she is."

"Did you see the music box she gave me?"

Michael nodded, grateful that some of the child's earlier excitement seemed to return.

"It's a carousel. It was Dr. Bennett's when she was a little girl. Her grandmother gave it to her. It plays a real pretty song. Dr. Bennett said it's a love song and..."

Surprised that Amanda had given Summer a childhood keepsake, Michael was moved by her generosity. "You know, honey, it was very nice of Dr. Bennett to give you the carousel, but I bet it has a lot of sentimental value for her if it was a gift from her grandmother. Maybe you should offer to return it."

Summer's expression fell. "But, Uncle Mike, she wanted me to have it. She said so. Besides, she has lots of others."

Michael arched a brow in question.

"It's true. She told me so. She collects them."

"She collects music boxes?"

"Mmm-hmm. Carousel ones. She said carousels are her weak... her weak..."

"Her weakness?" Michael offered.

"Yes." Summer grinned. "She likes them. That's why she goes to the Carousel House at the park all the time. She even has a favorite horse."

So, Amanda was fond of carousels, Michael thought, surprised and yet pleased at the thought of her being whimsical about painted horses. He tucked the information away.

"Do you think we could go see the Carousel House? Dr. Bennett said it's beautiful."

"Sure. Why not."

"When can we go?" Summer asked.

"How about tomorrow?"

"Yes!" Summer practically jumped up and down in her seat.

And perhaps while he was there, he would figure out some way to break through Amanda's defenses. Because, as Dave had warned him, time was running out.

Dinner tonight. Seven o'clock. I won't take no for an answer.

Amanda Bennett stared at the note once more and the bold, arrogant strokes that formed the name Michael. She looked up at the exquisite vase of flowers that had accompanied the card. Unable to resist, she reached out and fingered the delicate petal of one violet.

Brilliant purple, red and yellow blooms spilled from the crystal vase sitting on her coffee table, creating a wild, untamed effect. Something about the reckless, undisciplined explosion of color appealed to her.

It also reminded her of Michael.

Disturbed by how often the man had been invading her thoughts lately, Amanda frowned. She ran her fingertips along the edges of the card. Since Summer's birthday party, he'd been relentless, asking her out, sending flowers, balloons and nonsensical gifts. Even Gracie had commented, without bothering to hide her amusement, at Michael's visits and calls to the school office.

Amanda thought for a moment of the way he had been looking at her during their consultation meeting the day before. There had been such an intensity in his expression, a deep hunger in his navy eyes, every female fiber in her had responded to the sexual pull. She'd found herself wanting him to kiss her again, to hold her in his arms.

She was a romantic idiot, Amanda chided herself, hating herself for weakening. She tore the card in two and tossed it on the table. Turning her back to the flowers, she crossed the room and flipped on the stereo, filling the room with the sounds of Brahms. She *would not* go out with him again, she vowed as she dropped down onto the couch. Michael Grayson was going to *have* to take no for an answer.

Satisfied by her decision, Amanda tried to relax. She stretched out on the soft cushions. Hugging one of the pillows to her chest, she promised herself she wouldn't think about him anymore. But as her eyes closed and she drifted off to sleep, it was Michael who filled her thoughts.

When she opened her eyes again, it was to the sound of Michael's voice calling her name, to the feel of his fingers touching her cheek.

Amanda sat up with a start, wondering if she were still dreaming.

"Welcome back, Sleeping Beauty."

"Michael," she managed, her heartbeat quickening at the sight of him sitting in the chair next to her. She clutched the pillow to her. "What are you doing here?"

"Watching you sleep."

Quickly Amanda glanced around the room to assure herself she was indeed at home. She was. But Michael was here, too. She sat up straighter. "How did you get in here? The doors were locked."

"Any ten-year-old with a hairpin could have opened your front door. When you didn't answer, I went to the window. I saw you on the couch. You were tossing and turning so much I was worried you might be ill, so I let myself in." He gave her a sheepish smile. "For some reason, you've never struck me as a woman who napped during the day."

She wasn't, but obviously the week of restless nights brought on by Michael's pursuit of her, had taken its toll.

"Of course, one look at your face and I realized you were only dreaming. Then you settled down and looked so peaceful, I hated to wake you."

His voice sounded almost tender, Amanda thought as she returned the pillow she'd been clutching to the couch.

"But I knew if I let you sleep any longer, we'd be late."

"Late?" Amanda blinked. "Late for what?"

"For dinner," he said matter-of-factly. "Didn't you get my note? I sent one with the flowers."

Fighting back the guilty flush that climbed her cheeks, Amanda's eyes darted to the torn note lying on the table.

"I see that you did." He frowned. His gaze moved from the torn note back to her. "Evidently you weren't planning to go."

Amanda stood and smoothed the folds of her khaki-colored skirt. She looked into his eyes, disturbed by the emotion she saw in their blue depths. "No, I wasn't."

Standing, Michael moved over to the table and picked up the discarded note. The white oxford shirt stretched across his stiff back, the muscles bunched and tensed in his neck and shoulders. He crumpled the invitation in his fist, then dropped it beside the vase. His anger was palatable; yet when he turned, his face was inscrutable.

"I'll make you a deal, Amanda. Have dinner with me tonight and when the evening's over, if you still insist you don't want to see me again, that you feel nothing for me, then I promise to walk out of your life and never bother you again."

He crossed over to her and looked into her eyes. "One evening is all I'm asking, then you call the shots. What have you got to lose?"

Plenty, Amanda thought fifteen minutes later as Michael led her down the path of oak trees into City Park. The branches of the ancient oaks, draped in Spanish moss, swayed slightly in the evening breeze. "Michael, what are we doing here?" Her voice was a loud whisper in the silence.

"Going to dinner," he said. He pushed open the wrought-iron gate.

Amanda stepped into the garden entrance and the sweet, familiar scent of jasmine greeted her, bringing a smile to her lips. Even in the dying light of day, she could make out the interlacing of brick walks, the gnarled branches of the huge trees. She'd covered every inch of these gardens on her visits to the park's Carousel Pavilion. Twisted shapes and shadows from the trees played in the thickening darkness; but instead of fear she felt only the comfort of old friends.

Still, she protested, "Michael, I don't think we should be here. We'll get in trouble."

He chuckled. "What makes you think that?"

"Because the park's closed," she pointed out the obvious. She had visited the place often enough to know it wasn't open to the public after five and that they were trespassing.

"To the rest of the city, maybe. But not to us. I told you, we're having dinner here."

"I don't remember there being any restaurants here."

"That's because there aren't any." They moved down the tree-laden walkway lit only by the last of the fading sun and an occasional safety light. They stopped in front of the entrance to Story Land, the children's amusement area, now silent except for the faint rustle of leaves and the scurrying of squirrels in the huge oaks.

"Come on," he said, putting his arm around her shoulders. "There's something I want you to see."

The sun had completed its descent, casting shadows and a soft pink hue across the amusement rides. Strange, Amanda thought, to be here under the cloak of darkness without the laughter and squeals of children, without the noise and music.

Michael stopped. "This is what I wanted you to see," he said gently, pointing to the Carousel Pavilion.

The warmth of his breath tickled her ear, causing her pulse to race. Taking a steadying breath, Amanda took in the sight of the large white structure poised majestically against the dark canvas of night. Soft golden light spilled from the doors and stained-glass windows that encircled the house, delineating its three-tiered copper roof and twelve-sided shape. Although she'd been here dozens of times, never had she seen the Pavilion at night. "It's beautiful," she said, but found the word inadequate to describe the picture before her.

He gave her shoulders a light squeeze. "Summer told me how much you liked this place."

Liked? She loved the Carousel Pavilion...had from the first moment she'd seen it. It had always seemed such a magical place, a place where one could almost believe dreams and fairy tales really did come true.

"I thought you might enjoy seeing it at night."

Amanda swallowed, moved by his thoughtfulness. "Thank you."

After a moment Michael said, "I don't know about you, but I'm starved. Come on." He reached for her hand. "Let's go eat."

"But where?"

"Inside," he said, urging her toward the Pavilion.

She allowed him to lead her up the familiar wooden steps, across the wide deck with its mahogany-trimmed handrails and through the pane-glass doors. Once inside, she stopped and stared, enchanted all over again.

Wreathed in lights, the carousel turned slowly on its axis like a glittering, twirling gem. Painted horses, their manes windswept, their bodies captured in flight, were anchored to brass poles. Twin horses looked back from the sparkling beveled mirrors as they slowly glided up and down the rods to the sweet reedy sound of the calliope. Amanda's gaze rested on the dove gray stallion. Raised on its haunches, its silver mane lifted in the air as though caught in a gust of wind, he'd been her favorite from the first time she'd seen him.

"Magnificent, isn't it? The artists who did the restoration did a terrific job."

"Yes, they did."

"Why don't we eat dinner and then we can take a closer look."

Amanda shifted her attention from the carousel to the direction Michael indicated. A blue-and-white checked cloth lay spread on the floor with coordinating napkins, wineglasses and dinnerware for two. A large wicker hamper sat nearby.

"Remember I asked you to go with me on a picnic last Sunday?"

Amanda nodded, recalling how tempted she had been to accept his offer.

"Since you weren't able to get away then," he said, leading her to the makeshift table, "I thought we could have our picnic now."

Amanda dropped to her knees and tucked her feet beneath her, grateful for the fullness of her skirt.

Shaking out a linen napkin, Michael draped it across her lap then sat down next to her. "I wasn't sure what you liked, so I ordered some of my favorites. I hope you're hungry." He opened the lid on the basket and began emptying its contents. "Let's see, we've got fried chicken, potato salad..." Peeling off the top of another square bin, he peered inside. "Deviled eggs, stuffed mushrooms..."

Bemused, Amanda sat back and studied the strong lines of his face, the tiny laugh creases at the corners of his eyes. Strange, she thought as he continued to empty the hamper. She hadn't envisioned Michael as a man inclined toward romantic gestures. Yet, that's exactly what this had been. And to have picked the Carousel Pavilion of all places.

"There's supposed to be a bottle of wine in here someplace." He dug in the basket. "Ah. Here it is." Unwrapping the bottle, he uncorked it expertly and filled their glasses.

Amanda took a sip. "Hmm. Very nice," she said, enjoying the fine, dry Chablis.

Smiling, Michael handed her a plate. "If you think the wine's good, wait until you taste the chicken. It's terrific."

He was right, Amanda decided twenty minutes later. The chicken had been terrific, as had been the rest of the meal, the wine, and especially Michael's company.

Relaxed, she allowed him to refill her glass. Holding it up to the light, she smiled as the carousel's reflection bounced off her glass.

"You should see your face right now. You look like a kid in a toy store."

"When I come here, I feel like one," she said, tipping her head back and laughing.

"If I could, I'd buy this place for you just to see you smile like that every day."

Something in the deep, husky tone of his voice touched her like a caress, sending tingles of awareness skipping down her spine. Amanda cut a glance to where he lay stretched out on his side, propped up on one elbow sipping his wine. Lifting her gaze to meet his, her heartbeat quickened at the heated look in his blue eyes.

Disturbed by her own response, Amanda looked away. Setting down her glass, she pulled her knees up to her chest and hugged them to her. "Tell me about your sister," she said, deliberately changing the subject.

"My sister?" he asked, as though perplexed.

"Yes. What was she like?"

Michael paused a moment. "She was very kind, very gentle. And naive. She trusted people too easily."

Amanda caught the edge in his voice, the hard look in his eyes.

"Summer's a lot like Sara, except I think maybe she's stronger emotionally. At least, I hope so." He stared down into his wine, his thoughts obviously elsewhere.

There was a sadness, a loneliness about him that tore at Amanda, made her long to offer comfort. "Don't worry, Michael. Summer's a bright little girl and a lot stronger than you think. Most children are. You'd be surprised at how resilient kids can be."

"You're probably right." Taking a long drink of his wine, Michael studied the perfect oval of her face, her creamy skin warmed by the glow of soft lights. He moved his gaze to the curve of her lips, bare except for the shimmer of wine.

"It's getting late," she said, the wary look back in her eyes. She sat up and started to repack the hamper. "We probably should be going."

Michael grabbed her wrist; her pulse scrambled beneath his thumb. "Not yet," he said. Easing his hold on her wrist, he slid his palm against hers. "Don't you want to ride the carousel?"

Her gaze shifted to the painted horses, sliding up and down as they turned in a slow circle.

Catching the look of yearning in her eyes, Michael seized the moment. "Come on." Quickly, he came to his feet and pulled her up beside him. "Show me which horse is your favorite. Summer told me you had one."

"But—"

"No buts, Amanda. Not tonight." Threading his fingers through hers, he urged her toward the carousel. He jumped onto the platform and pulled her up beside him. For a moment he just stood there, acutely aware of her body, soft and warm against him.

He heard the slight catch in her breath before she stepped back and pulled her hand free. "My favorite one's over there," she said. Turning, she weaved her way through the moving horses.

Slowly, Michael followed, watching as Amanda turned from one to another of the painted horses as though reacquainting herself with old friends. She stopped beside a gray-colored steed. The horse's head was held high, his legs thrust forward. A jewel-encrusted saddle adorned his back. Amanda ran her fingers lovingly along his silver mane.

For a moment Michael envied the wooden horse. He wondered what it would be like to be on the receiving end of Amanda's affection. "What do you call him?"

Her fingers stilled. She glanced up, her gaze tangling with his.

"Summer said you had named him. But even if she hadn't, I would've guessed as much. He's obviously very special to you."

"I call him Sultan," she said softly.

"Sultan," Michael repeated. He looked from Amanda's cautious face to the painted horse. "Why Sultan?"

The corners of her mouth curved slightly. "Because he's surrounded by females."

Michael glanced to the right and then to the left, noting the horses on either side were smaller, their saddles painted in shades of pale pink and yellow with floral patterns woven in the grain. "You know, I think you're right."

She gazed wistfully at the wooden stallion for another moment, then turned to Michael. "It's getting late. We really should be going."

But he didn't want to go—not yet. "Aren't you going to ride Sultan?"

Amanda looked at the large horse, moving up and down on the brass pole, then down at her skirt. "I'm not exactly dressed for riding."

Michael ran his gaze down her trim figure, noting the way the thin white blouse skimmed her breasts and nipped in at the waist of her full skirt. "Sure you are." Stepping forward, he encircled her waist with his hands and when the horse edged down the pole, he lifted her onto the saddle. "If ever a woman looked like she belonged on an English side saddle, it's you."

She did look like she belonged on a side saddle, Michael decided. Stepping back, he leaned against a stationary chariot and studied her. She reminded him of a princess, he thought, noting her straight back, the proud tilt of her chin. Yet, atop the flying horse with her hair loose, her lips bare, she seemed somehow more gentle, more vulnerable than she had before.

She gave him a soft, easy smile. "Did you know the tails on these horses are all made of real horse hair?" She caught a handful and let it fall through her fingers.

"You don't say," Michael returned, enjoying the sound of her voice, the way her eyes glistened like sherry.

"It's true. And this carousel is one of the last of its kind in the country."

Amanda explained the history of the carousel, how with time and the ever-changing economy, most had been neglected and eventually dismantled and sold to collectors. But Michael barely heard any of it. He was more intrigued by the way her mouth moved as she spoke, the way her small pink tongue darted out to wet her lips.

"I hate to think that maybe someday they might all be gone. Can you imagine a world without the magic of the carousel?"

"No, I can't," Michael said, looking at the woman before him.

The calliope ground out the final notes of its tune and the carousel came to a halt. The laughter faded from her eyes. "It's getting late. I really do need to be going."

Amanda shifted, bracing herself on the saddle as she started to dismount. Instinctively, Michael reached for her. Her eyes grew wide and he heard her draw in her breath as he captured her around the waist. Slowly, gently, he eased her to the floor.

Unable to resist, Michael dipped his head and brushed his lips against hers. Her mouth was soft and warm beneath his own. He tasted the trace of wine, the laughter that lingered on her lips.

And the sweet promise of passion as she pressed her mouth to his.

Pulse racing, Michael lifted his head and looked into her eyes glazed with awareness, at her lips moist and inviting. He couldn't think about plans, about custody suits. Right now all he could concentrate on was feeding his need for more of her warmth, more of her softness.

She slipped her arms around his neck, drawing him to her. And when he would have taken her mouth again, she offered it to him, parting her lips.

The tip of her tongue touched his and Michael's control broke. Giving in to the passion and need he'd kept in check for weeks, he took all that she offered.

And found he still wanted more.

Five

Michael kissed Amanda once more, then set her away from him while he still could. Turning, he braced one arm against the wall of Amanda's doorway and drew a deep, gulping breath as he fought the ache in his lower body.

Stopping with just a kiss at her front door had been every bit as hard as it had been to hold himself to only kisses at the Carousel Pavilion.

On second thought, maybe it was harder, he decided. A soft breeze whispered through the night carrying the clean scent of freshly cut grass. Lifting his head, he looked out across the lawn.

All during dinner he'd found it impossible to think about the custody suit, Martha Winthrop, or his reasons for seeking out Amanda in the first place. And now it was even worse. Now all he could think of was how much he wanted to lie with her on the earth's carpet, beneath the shadow of the magnolia tree, its branches heavy with fragrant blooms, with only the soft light of the moon touching her skin. His body hardened once more and he squeezed his eyes shut to block out the erotic images.

"Michael?"

Taking another deep breath, Michael gave himself a mental shake before turning to face Amanda. Bathed in the glow of the porch light, her skin resembled cream satin, her pale hair expensive silk. He smoothed a strand away from her cheek and her dark eyes grew even darker.

"Would you like to come in for coffee?" she asked, her voice husky.

"If I come in, I'll want more than coffee and I don't think you're quite ready for that." He paused. "Or am I wrong?"

She hesitated a moment, her eyes searching his. "No," she whispered before dropping her gaze.

"It's okay," he said, tipping up her chin. A strange tenderness spread through him, easing the ache inside him. He didn't want her to be embarrassed, didn't want to see the light go out of her eyes.

He brushed his thumb across her bottom lip, all pink and swollen from his kisses.

She trembled and closed her eyes at his touch.

"I want us to both be sure." Michael heard himself saying the words and wondered if he were ten kinds of a fool. How could she be so responsive and yet so totally unaware of her own passion? But suddenly, seducing her, carrying through on his plan, was no longer enough. He wanted Amanda to want him—as much as he wanted her.

"I guess I'll say good-night." Amanda stepped back. "I had a wonderful time tonight. Thank you."

Reluctant to say goodbye, he said, "There's a big charity affair tomorrow night. The Zoo To-Do. It's a benefit thing for the zoo. Everybody who's anybody in New Orleans turns out for it. Would you like to go?" In truth, he hadn't planned to attend. He usually avoided the star-studded event that attracted so many of the city's blue bloods. He had simply bought the tickets to support the fund-raiser.

"I'd like that," she said softly.

"Great. I'll pick you up at seven." Michael smiled, feeling some of the tension leave him. After giving her a quick kiss, he headed down the walk.

Once inside, Amanda leaned against the door and hugged her arms around herself. She smiled, feeling as though she'd been dreaming. The entire evening had been wonderful, magical—the romantic picnic, the unexpected visit to the Carousel Pavilion, being in Michael's arms.

She squeezed her eyes shut remembering the thrill of his kisses, the feel of his body pressed so intimately next to hers. A warm ache spread through her, rekindling desires she'd buried so deeply during her marriage, desires that had remained dormant—until Michael.

Remember what happened the last time, a voice inside her warned.

And suddenly the old doubts began to resurface. Opening her eyes, Amanda walked into the living room, trying to escape the painful memories of Adam's confession, his futile apologies.

Her gaze was immediately drawn to the flowers—Michael's flowers. As she started to withdraw one dark red rose from the arrangement, she pricked her finger on a thorn.

Muttering an oath at the sharp stab of pain, she brought the tip of her finger to her mouth and sucked. Carefully she removed the rose with her other hand and sank to the couch.

She sniffed the flower's sweetness, then drew the velvety petals across her cheek and thought about Michael. He *wasn't* like Adam, she told herself. It was *her* he was interested in, not her suitability as a mother for his niece. He'd given her no reason to believe otherwise. And yet...

Amanda sighed, disgusted with herself for being unable to squelch the seeds of doubt. Maybe Gracie was right. It was time she let go of the past...time she learned to trust again. Not every man was like Adam. She had no reason to believe that Michael would lie to her, use her as Adam had done.

Still, all through the night and the next day that voice inside her persisted, some instinct had her wondering if she weren't making another mistake.

By the time seven o'clock arrived the following evening, Amanda was as nervous as a schoolgirl going to her first high school prom.

But when she opened her front door, the attack of nerves was forgotten as her eyes feasted on Michael. He'd caught her eye when he'd been wearing a sport coat and slacks. He'd made her pulse beat faster when he'd been dressed in jeans and an oxford cloth shirt. But the sight of him standing in her doorway in a formal black tux, his white shirt set off by onyx button covers and matching cuff links, made her head spin.

"Hi." He smiled that sexy little grin and Amanda's mouth went dry.

"Hello," she managed to get out.

"You look beautiful," he said, his eyes caressing her as he spoke.

"Thanks. You look pretty handsome yourself."

"According to Summer, I look like the groom on the top of a wedding cake."

"Must be the tie." Amanda smiled, relaxing under his good humor. She picked up her evening bag.

"I should have known you females would stick together." He extended his arm. "All set?"

"Yes."

By the time they reached the Audubon Zoo, Amanda wasn't sure she'd said one intelligible thing during the entire fifteen-minute drive.

"I think we go in over there." Michael pointed to a large group of people milling around the entrance gate.

Amanda allowed him to guide her through the din of elegantly dressed guests, far too conscious of his hand at her back. Once inside, the crowd thinned somewhat and Michael shifted his hand to her waist.

"I see what you mean about this being 'the' place to be seen," Amanda said, spotting a number of the city's politicians and social figures. "Isn't that the governor over there?"

"Probably. Everybody wants to be sure their name makes it in the society column."

"What about you?" Amanda asked, slanting him a glance.

"I believe in supporting the Zoo and the animal shelters, that's why I buy tickets to this thing every year. But I couldn't care less whether my name gets in the newspaper or not."

"Then why did you come? Why not just give the tickets away?"

"I usually do," Michael informed her.

"But not this time?"

"No. Not this time." Michael stopped and looked into her eyes. "I wanted to be with you and I thought if I asked you to a charitable benefit, it would be harder for you to say no."

It had been difficult to say no to him, but it had had nothing to do with the benefit, Amanda admitted.

"Hello, Michael. How are you?" A handsome couple with silvering hair and matching warm smiles stopped beside them.

"Dr. Duncan, Mrs. Duncan. Good to see you," Michael said.

After introductions were made, she and Michael continued to move among the guests, pausing periodically while Michael exchanged greetings and introduced her to his friends and acquaintances.

Michael proved a fun and knowledgeable escort. "And the brunette over there, the one poured into that red beaded thing..." He pointed to a striking woman with long black hair and a magnificent figure shown off to perfection in a fitted evening dress. "She owns a nightclub on Bourbon Street."

And her club must be doing well, Amanda thought, noting the size of the diamonds sparkling at the woman's ears and neck. Amanda glanced around, surprised at the haute couture designs many of the women were wearing. "I don't think I've seen this much glitter since I went to one of the Mardi Gras balls."

"People in New Orleans like nothing better than dressing up for a party."

Amanda laughed as they turned the corner of the walk-way. "And to think I was worried I would be overdressed."

Michael paused and focused his full attention on Amanda. Slowly, he moved his gaze over her indigo-colored silk dress, making her acutely aware of the deep slit up the back and the peeks of bare skin the opening afforded.

His eyes darkened and for a second Amanda was unable to breathe. Her skin burned as though brushed by a flame. Her nipples puckered beneath the silk and Amanda could almost feel Michael's touch.

"Believe me. There's not a thing wrong with the way you look."

"Thank you," Amanda managed, unable to look away. Her heart continued its wild race.

"Mike Grayson. Son of a gun, I thought that was you. I was just saying to Ellen . . ."

Michael turned at the sound of the man's voice and Amanda's body went limp as the moment was broken.

Twenty minutes and a half dozen introductions later, Amanda's heart rate had returned to normal. As they continued along the tree-lined pathway, she relaxed. Enjoying the sight of the tiny white lights scattered amid the majestic oaks, she recalled the previous night and the way the lights of the carousel had sparkled in the moonlight.

They stopped at the large fish pond and Amanda admired the beautiful teal-colored cockatoo perched on its trainer's shoulder.

"You're supposed to be impressed by the bird, not the handler," Michael whispered in her ear.

"Any reason I can't be impressed by both?" His warm breath fanned her neck, sending a delicious shudder down her spine. Amanda cut a glance up at him out of the corner of her eye.

"Yes."

She lifted one brow.

He caught her fingers, brought them to his lips and kissed their tips. "Tonight the only man I want you to be impressed by is me."

The deep, husky sound of his voice, the hungry look in his eyes, sent a burst of pleasure through her. "You don't have to worry. I'm impressed." In fact, she was more than impressed. She was well on her way to falling in love with him.

Unnerved by the realization and the effect his nearness was having on her, Amanda turned away. She looked toward another path in search of diversion from Michael, from her feelings for him. Taking a deep breath, she caught the tantalizing scent of simmering spices. She sniffed again. "Hmm. What's that wonderful smell?"

Michael smiled. "Why don't we find out?"

He led her to another clearing filled with more than a dozen tables draped in pristine white cloths, each sporting large warming trays and serving dishes piled high with food. Cardboard tents with the names of some of the city's finest eating establishments rested on each tabletop. "Most of the better restaurants donate one of their specialty dishes for tonight's affair." He looked at her and asked, "Hungry?"

Her mouth watered as the delicious aromas reminded her just how long it had been since she'd eaten. "Yes. I am," Amanda replied.

"Anything special you'd like to try?" Michael took her past one row of tables.

"I don't know." She laughed. Each dish looked better than the last. "Everything! It all smells wonderful."

Michael laughed, too. "It is." He walked over to one of the steaming dishes. "If you're feeling adventuresome, I recommend the crawfish *étouffé.*"

Amanda studied the tomato-colored sauce with chunks of crawfish being served over a bed of fluffy white rice. "I'm not sure I'm ready for that much adventure."

"I knew that conservative Bostonian was going to show up sooner or later." He grinned, effectively quelling any possible sting from his words before guiding her to another table. "How about the fettuccine Alfredo? It should be a safe bet."

Conservative. Safe. Funny, she didn't feel any of those things when she was with Michael. In fact, she felt anything but safe and conservative.

"Amanda? Do you want to try the fettuccine?" Michael asked, his gaze questioning.

Just then the waiter at the next station lifted the lid on a large pot of steaming gumbo. Amanda caught a whiff of the unique blend of onions, sweet peppers, celery, tomatoes and garlic simmering in a thick sauce with shrimp and okra. The cayenne pepper tickled her nose, but she couldn't resist. "I think I'll try the gumbo instead."

"It's hot," Michael warned.

"I think I can handle it."

"I take back what I said about you being conservative." He raised two fingers for the waiter.

By the time Amanda had eaten the last morsel of rice in her bowl, she'd also finished two full glasses of ice water. "I can't believe how thirsty I am." She licked the last few drops from her lips and set the cup on the small table she and Michael were sharing.

Michael chuckled. "It's all that cayenne in the gumbo. You're not used to it. Wait here, I'll get you a refill." Taking her glass, he headed toward one of the two bars set up in the clearing.

Feeling more relaxed and happier than she had in a long time, Amanda shifted her gaze to the chattering guests. She smiled at the sight of two society matrons preening before one of the local newscasters.

"Amanda? Amanda Bennett, is that you?"

Amanda turned her head and spotted the elegant gray-haired woman approaching. She came to her feet. "Mrs. Winthrop, it's so good to see you again."

The woman pulled a pained expression. "I thought I asked you to call me Martha. Mrs. Winthrop sounds so old." Smiling, she took Amanda's hand into hers and squeezed it. "Besides, your mother and I were practically like sisters in college and I simply won't hear of Elinore's little girl calling me Mrs. Winthrop. Understood?"

"Understood."

"Now tell me, how are you, dear? It's been months since I've seen you."

"I'm fine, thanks."

Releasing her hand, Martha took a step back and surveyed Amanda. "Well, I must say you certainly look wonderful. New Orleans must agree with you."

"It does," Amanda admitted, smiling. She couldn't help but wonder how much credit Michael Grayson deserved for her present happiness. "I love the city, the people. I feel like . . . like I belong here."

Martha laughed. "I'm not sure your mother would be pleased to hear you say that. The last time I spoke with her, she and your father were missing you a great deal."

"I miss them, too," Amanda said, feeling a slight twinge of guilt. Her parents hadn't been at all happy about her divorce and had liked the idea of her moving so far away even less. But Boston held too many reminders, too many remnants of dreams that had shattered. "I'm hoping they'll come visit me during the Christmas holidays."

Martha raised one perfectly arched brow. "Sounds like you really are here to stay."

"I am," Amanda said, and realized it was true. New Orleans had been a temporary sanctuary for her after her divorce, but somewhere along the way it had become home.

"Well, then, we'll both have to twist your mother's arm a bit and get her to come down for a visit. I haven't seen her in years. We've got a lot of catching up to do."

"I'm sure Mother would love it."

"Here's your wine, Aunt Martha." Amanda looked over at the tall man with dark blond hair who came to stand beside Martha. In his mid-thirties, Amanda guessed, noting the strong resemblance between them. His white dinner jacket set off his deep golden tan beautifully. Years of habit, born from studying and assessing potential campaign donors in Boston's political circle, had Amanda guessing at the designer and the price.

"Thank you, dear." Martha took the glass of white wine from him. "Bradley, I don't believe you've met Amanda Bennett. She's the daughter of my friend Elinore, the school friend from Boston that I told you about." She turned toward Amanda. "Amanda, my nephew, Bradley Winthrop."

Bradley took her hand in his. He smiled at her; his eyes, a striking shade of green, crinkled at the corners. "Hello," he said warmly.

"How do you do?"

"Now that I've met you, much much better," he said.

He was handsome, Amanda admitted, and obviously a charmer. She withdrew her hand. "Thank you, Mr. Winthrop."

"Bradley," he corrected with another smile. "May I call you Amanda?"

"Yes, of course."

"Will you be visiting New Orleans long? I'd love to show you around the city."

"Actually, I'm not a visitor. I live here."

"Amanda moved here last fall," Martha informed him. "Don't you remember my mentioning it to you?"

"You mean this gorgeous creature has been living in the same city with me and I'm just now meeting her?"

Amanda couldn't help but laugh at the crushed expression on his face. Yes, Bradley Winthrop was definitely a charmer. But he didn't make her heart race or her pulse beat faster—not the way Michael did.

"Behave yourself, Bradley. You were away on one of your little sailing adventures when Amanda arrived. Otherwise, you'd have met her sooner."

"If you had told me your old school friend had such a beautiful daughter, I would have cut my trip short and come home."

"Ignore him, Amanda. Instead of taking over his father's business, sometimes I think Bradley should have gone on the stage."

"I'm sure he would have done quite well," Amanda said, grinning at Bradley's pained expression.

"Anyway, I'm ashamed to admit that I haven't called this dear child in months to even see how she's been getting along. When you and I talked last, I believe you said you were taking some sort of classes."

"Yes. Refresher courses. At the University of New Orleans. I'm hoping to take the state exam this fall and get my license to practice in Louisiana."

"Practice?" Bradley asked. "Are you a doctor?"

"A child psychologist," Amanda explained.

"Amanda worked for a very reputable firm in Boston before her marriage," Martha informed her nephew.

"You're married?" Bradley asked, his show of disappointment almost comical.

"Divorced," Amanda said, hating the failure the word implied.

Bradley brightened. "In that case, I hope you're planning to stay in New Orleans for a while."

"I am, provided I can get on with one of the clinics."

"Maybe Aunt Martha can help. She sits on a number of the hospital boards. Don't you, Aunt Martha?"

"Bradley's right, dear. And of course, I'd be glad to send a letter of recommendation for you," Martha added. "Do you have a particular clinic in mind?"

"Not at the moment." Although she appreciated the offer, Amanda didn't want any favors. That had been part of the reason she'd come to New Orleans. Here she was simply Amanda Bennett, not Ambassador Bennett's daughter or somebody important's wife. And any job she got was going to be on her own merit, Amanda vowed.

"Well, let me know if I can help. I'd be happy to put in a word for you," Martha said.

"Thanks. I'll keep that in mind. But right now, I'm concentrating on getting through the next four weeks of classes. Then I'll have to wait until the fall to take the exam."

Bradley grimaced. "I certainly don't envy you. I'm sure you'll be glad to get all that behind you and start working again."

"Yes, I will. But, actually, I am working now. With a group of children at Saint Margaret's. Of course, it's only in a volunteer capacity, but I enjoy it."

"Saint Margaret's." Martha took a sip of her wine. She drew her brows together. "I don't seem to recall any Saint Margaret's clinic or hospital. Where is this place located?"

"It's uptown. But it's not a clinic or a hospital. It's a Catholic grade school. I've been doing some counseling there a few afternoons a week."

Martha's face paled. "The little school off of State Street?"

"Yes. That's it."

Martha's hand shook slightly as she set her wineglass down on the table. "Do you work with all of the children there?"

"No," Amanda responded, puzzled. "Just the ones whose parents or teachers have recommended them for counseling."

"You mean, the problem kids," Bradley said, scorn in his voice.

"I wouldn't call them 'problem kids'," Amanda informed him, frowning. She wondered then how she could have thought him charming. "Sometimes the children are just afraid or they might be having trouble adjusting to a new environment."

"Tell me, Amanda. Would you happen to have come across a little girl there by the name of Summer Grayson?" Martha's voice was calm, but she seemed tense, edgy. "She's seven years old and in the third grade. A pretty little thing with long black hair and green eyes."

Suddenly uneasy, Amanda looked from Bradley's scowling face to Martha's anxious one. For some reason she was reluctant to tell them anything about Summer. "Martha, you know a doctor can't reveal anything about her patients," she said, trying to sound light.

Bradley narrowed his eyes. "Then the Grayson kid *is* one of your patients?"

Just then Amanda looked past Bradley and spotted Michael heading toward her. Relief flooded through her. "Michael," she said, ignoring Bradley's last question. "I was beginning to think you'd gotten lost."

Michael swallowed, trying to ease the thick knot of anger and panic that had lodged in his throat at the sight of Amanda with the Winthrops. "No. Just a long line at the bar." He flicked his gaze over Bradley and Martha. "Here's your Perrier."

Amanda took the glass of sparkling water. "Thank you." She moved to his side. "Michael, I'd like to introduce you to Martha Winthrop and her nephew, Bradley. Martha and my mother were roommates in college. Martha, Bradley, this is my friend, Michael Grayson."

"The Winthrops and I are already acquainted," Michael informed her.

Martha's chin tilted up slightly. Her eyes flashed. "Yes. Michael and I share . . . a mutual interest."

"You and I share nothing," Michael said fiercely, angry at Martha's implication that they shared Summer. They didn't. Summer belonged to him.

"I didn't realize you knew Michael, Amanda. Tell me, dear, how did you two happen to meet?"

"Yeah, Amanda." Bradley leaned nonchalantly against a tree. His gaze raked lazily over Amanda. "How'd a classy lady like you get tangled up with a guy like Grayson?"

Amanda gasped.

Michael clenched his fists at his side. He took a step toward Bradley, wanting to wipe that smug look off his pretty-boy face. "Another crack like that, Winthrop, and you'll find yourself paying a visit to your dentist before the evening's over."

Bradley straightened. His mocking smile disappeared. "Maybe you've got the rest of the people in this town falling for that 'tough guy' and 'poor boy makes good' image of yours, but I don't. I'm not afraid of you because I know what you really are. You're still Crazy Alice Grayson's punk kid."

"Bradley!" Martha glared at her nephew. "That's enough. You've had too much to drink and you're making a scene."

Michael grabbed Bradley by the lapels of his jacket, crushing the expensive silk. It had been years since anyone had taunted him with that hated name the kids had labeled his poor, sick mother. Yet the mere mention of it made him feel twelve years old again and all the old hurt and anger came back.

"Michael, don't." Amanda tugged at his arm. "Please."

He looked down at Amanda, her face drained of color, her dark brown eyes wide with concern. He glanced to his left, noting the small group of people watching. "Be grateful I've learned some manners, Winthrop. Twenty years ago I wouldn't have given a damn about ruining this little party. I'd have broken you into tiny pieces. Come anywhere near me or what's mine again, and I will."

Shoving Bradley away from him, he turned to Amanda. "Let's get out of here."

Six

___

"**I**'m coming inside," Michael told Amanda as she unlocked the front door. "We need to talk."

"By all means," Amanda said, leading the way. She had a few questions of her own for Mr. Michael Grayson. Like, what had happened between Bradley and him to cause the other man to be so rude? And how did Martha Winthrop know Summer? And why had the other woman been so interested in the child?

Amanda flipped on the light switch, bathing the living room in a soft white glow. After placing her evening clutch on the coffee table beside the vase of flowers, she turned to face Michael.

"Would you like something to drink?" she asked, trying to defuse the tension that had mushroomed between them during the silent drive home. "I don't have any beer, but I've got some wine."

"What? No brandy? That is what you blue bloods drink, isn't it?"

Amanda froze, taken aback by the underlying anger in his tone. His derision stung; but Amanda struggled to keep her voice calm. "I think I have a bottle that my father gave me. Since you were drinking beer at the party, I assumed that's what you prefer. But if you'd rather have brandy—"

"Forget it. I wouldn't want you to waste the good stuff on me. Save it for your friends," he said, his voice cold, his expression hard.

"I don't know why you're so angry, Michael. I'm not even sure who you're angry with. But I do know you have a real hang-up about what you perceive as social classes, and I don't like it."

"And you, my dear Amanda, have a nasty habit of playing shrink. You can save the analysis for somebody else." He tossed his coat onto a chair. "Right now, all I want from you are some straight answers."

Amanda smarted, stung by his harsh words. Answers? Was that what he wanted? Judging by the steamy looks he'd been giving her all evening, she had thought he'd wanted a great deal more.

At least, he had an hour ago—before they'd run into the Winthrops. She studied his face. The mouth that had been so gentle and inviting when he'd smiled at her was now pulled into a thin, angry line.

She sat down on the chair beside the sofa. "First of all, I think we'd better get something straight. I don't *owe* you any explanations. But I'm willing to answer your questions...provided you answer mine." She paused. "Is it a deal?"

Michael frowned, then muttered, "Deal."

"All right, what do you want to know?" Folding her arms, she leaned back.

"You can start by telling me what your connection is to the Winthrops."

Amanda stared up into his scowling face. His eyes that had been so filled with warmth and desire earlier were as cold and hard as steel.

"Are you going to answer me?"

Amanda's back stiffened. "Not until you sit down. I refuse to conduct this . . . this conversation—if you can call it that—with you standing there glaring at me like Attila the Hun."

Muttering, Michael dropped onto the couch across from her. "All right. Now, why don't you explain to me how it is you happen to be so chummy with the Winthrops."

"Chummy?" Amanda repeated. "I'd hardly say speaking with Martha and Bradley Winthrop constitutes 'chummy.' We're merely acquaintances."

"Dammit, Amanda. Forget the semantics. What's your connection to the Winthrops? How do you know them?"

"Martha Winthrop went to college with my mother. They were sorority sisters. When I moved to New Orleans, my mother called Martha and asked her to look in on me occasionally."

"And Bradley? Did your mother ask him to look in on you, too?"

Amanda blinked, surprised by the depth of his hostility. "I met him for the first time tonight. Michael, what's all this about? The two of you were practically at each other's throats. And Martha looked positively ill when she saw you. And she was asking me questions about Summer."

"What did she want to know?"

"I'm not sure exactly. When I told her I was working at Saint Margaret's, she asked me if I knew Summer."

"What did you tell her?"

"I didn't have a chance to tell her anything. That's when you came over and the whole conversation shifted."

Michael let out his breath and Amanda noticed for the first time that beneath the anger he was genuinely worried.

"Then she doesn't know about the problems Summer's been having? That she's needed counseling?"

"Not from me she doesn't. But what difference does it make?" Amanda asked, although she was beginning to suspect she knew the answer already. "Michael, will you please tell me what's going on?"

He looked up at her, his expression wary. "Haven't you figured it out yet?"

"I think so. But I'd still like to hear it from you."

Slowly, Michael straightened. He loosened the studs at his throat and rubbed the back of his neck. Dark swirls of hair curled at the opening of his white dress shirt. "Will you give me your promise that whatever I tell you stays between us— no matter what happens?"

"Yes," Amanda said, moistening her lips. She brought her eyes up to his face.

"Martha Winthrop is Summer's grandmother."

"But I thought..."

"You thought what I wanted you to think. That I'm Summer's only relative."

It was the eyes, Amanda decided as Michael confirmed what she'd started to suspect. Summer had Bradley's green eyes. "If Bradley is Summer's father, then why—"

"Bradley's not Summer's father!"

"But I thought—" Amanda paused. "Then who is?"

"Phillip Winthrop." The words were little more than a whisper, yet his voice sounded raw.

"Phillip?" She tried to recall where she'd heard the name before.

"Martha's son. He died before Summer was born."

Amanda swallowed, remembering her mother mentioning Martha's only child had been killed tragically. She tried to assimilate that with what Michael had told her about Summer's father. "You said Summer's father... Phillip— wouldn't marry your sister. Was it because he already had a wife?"

Michael laughed, the sound was empty, bitter. "No. Phillip wasn't married. And to be honest, I think he really did love my sister. God knows, she certainly loved him."

"Then why..."

"Because Sara wasn't good enough," he said through clenched teeth. "Phillip had that blue blood running through his veins. But Sara didn't. She wasn't some little debutante who went to all the right schools and took summer trips to Europe. Hell, even if I could have afforded to send her, she wouldn't have accepted. She couldn't trace her ancestors back to the *Mayflower* or whatever it is people like the Winthrops do to determine if someone's bloodlines are good enough."

Amanda's heart twisted a little as she imagined what a blow it must have been to Michael to see his sister rejected.

"She was common—just like me."

Michael lifted his eyes; they tangled with hers. Amanda could see the pain she heard in his voice and moved beside him.

She took his hands in hers and squeezed. "There's nothing common about you, Michael Grayson. I doubt any of the Graysons could ever be described that way."

"Martha Winthrop wouldn't agree with you. And you saw Bradley's reaction when he found out you were with me."

"Then Martha and Bradley Winthrop are fools. I was proud to be with you," she told him sincerely. "Any woman would be."

Michael's fingers tightened around hers. His eyes darkened to a smoky blue.

"I wouldn't have wanted to be with anyone else," she managed, despite her quickening pulse.

He made a noise that sounded like part sigh, part groan. Untangling their fingers, he slipped his arms around her, drawing her close. "Amanda." Her name sounded like a prayer on his lips.

Amanda swallowed. Her heart began to beat faster as he leaned closer, until all she could see was his face, his eyes, his mouth.

"You have no idea how much I've wanted to do this all evening."

But she did know, Amanda admitted silently, lifting her face for his kiss. Because she'd wanted—waited for—this moment, too.

His lips brushed her forehead, her temple. She closed her eyes and he kissed each of them. She took a quick breath, trying to stem the heat unfurling inside her. The faint scent of soap, of men's cologne, of the tree-filled park surrounded her until only the smell, the taste, the touch of Michael filled her senses. The flame, only banked since the previous night, leapt to life inside her.

When he pressed a kiss to the corner of her mouth, Amanda's control slipped. "Michael." She slid her arms up around his neck and pulled his mouth to hers.

He accepted her offering greedily. His tongue thrust past her open lips, hungrily seeking, tasting, deepening the kiss.

"So sweet. So very sweet," he whispered as he nipped at her ear, her neck.

Amanda whimpered. She leaned her head back as his mouth continued to pleasure and torment. Needs that had been buried burst to life inside her, building to a fever pitch.

Michael stared into her eyes, his own dark with hunger, and loosened the single button at the nape of her dress. The silk slithered down to her shoulders, pooling above her breasts.

Tenderly, almost reverently, he caressed her bare shoulder. "Such soft skin," he said, his voice husky. He drew a line with his finger from her shoulder to her throat, down to where the silk hovered above her breasts. "I've been going crazy wondering if you were this soft all over."

Her heart pounding furiously, Amanda arched her back as the need inside her grew even stronger. "Michael," she whispered his name, unsure just what it was she was asking for.

He hooked the silk with his finger and pulled, baring her breasts. She heard his breath catch, saw the desire burning in his eyes and a rush of pleasure shot through her.

He wanted her, truly wanted *her*—as a woman, not as a substitute for a loved one he'd lost or because his child needed a mother. He wanted her...for herself.

And she wanted him.

Michael touched her gently, his fingers unsteady as he explored the shape of each breast. He pinned her with his eyes as he cupped their fullness, brushed his thumb across their peaks. "Your skin feels like silk...warm, living silk."

Her nipples pebbled, begging for his touch. Michael obliged. He lowered his head and took one nipple in his mouth, laving, kissing, nipping at the sensitized flesh while his hand ministered to her other breast.

Heat seeped through her, flowing to the juncture between her thighs. Amanda freed her arms from her dress, then buried her fingers in his hair. She held him close and arched her body toward him, wanting, needing more.

When he pulled away for a moment, Amanda started to protest. Opening her eyes, the words stuck in her throat as he unfastened the remaining buttons of his shirt and pulled it free of his trousers. Amanda clutched a handful of silk skirt as she studied his bare chest, all tanned and muscled. Her fingers itched to trace the line of dark hair that ran down his flat stomach and disappeared into his slacks.

Michael reached for her hand, forcing her to relinquish her stranglehold on her dress. "Feel what you do to me," he said, placing her hand over his heart.

She touched the warm, muscled flesh. His heart beat out a frenetic tune beneath her fingertips. Excited, she gave in to impulse and began stroking his chest, weaving her fingers through the trail of dark hair that covered his skin.

Feeling bold, Amanda flicked her finger over his nipple.

Michael shuddered.

Heady with the knowledge that she excited him, Amanda dropped her head to his chest. She touched the tip of his nipple with her tongue.

Michael groaned. "Amanda." He tipped her face up and took her mouth, devouring, conquering, burning her with his kiss.

Amanda could sense the leashed power, the desire barely held in check, as he eased her back onto the cushions of the couch. The storm began to rage inside her as his hair-roughened chest pressed against her bare breasts. She lifted her hips to meet him, glorying in the feel of his maleness resting hard and heavy with desire against her.

Michael groaned again and deepened the kiss. Suddenly his hands were everywhere—in her hair, on her breasts, caressing her thighs.

When she saw the heated look in his eyes, Amanda gave
a silent prayer of thanks that she'd given in to the impulse
to wear the garter belt and hose.

His hand moved between her legs, near the center of her
warmth, and Amanda bit her lip to stop from crying out her
need.

He stroked her through the silk of her panties.

She gripped the edges of his shirt.

"Don't fight it, love."

The thin barrier seemed to make the intimacy more erotic.
Every muscle in her body was attuned to the rhythm of his
finger moving across the damp silk covering her feminine
secrets.

"You're so hot . . . like liquid fire," he whispered as he
continued to stoke the heat inside her. "That's it," he
coaxed. "Burn for me, Amanda. Burn for me, the way I've
been burning for you."

The flame burst inside her, engulfing her, and Amanda
clutched at his shoulders, digging her nails into his muscled
flesh as wave after wave of sensation washed over her.

"I knew it would be like this between us." He kissed her
mouth, her breasts, then drew a line with his tongue to her
navel.

Her stomach fluttered beneath the assault. Amanda
pulled his head back up so she could taste his mouth again.

She reached for the buckle of his belt.

"Yes," he whispered, his breath catching as her fingers
loosened the button of his slacks.

Amanda shivered at his response. Had she known, too, on
some elemental level that there would be passion like this
between them? Was that the reason she had been so unsure, so afraid of her feelings when she was with him?

She pulled down his zipper and stroked his hard length.

Michael's body stiffened and Amanda heard a guttural
sound, but wasn't sure if came from him or from her.

"I want you," he said, his voice filled with need.

Amanda stared into his eyes and for the first time in her
life she knew what the term "raw hunger" meant. "And I
want you."

Michael crushed her to him, touching, exploring. "Oh, Amanda. I can't believe I'm here with you at last. All these weeks, I've wanted you so much and tonight when I saw you with Bradley..."

He kissed her again, leaving her breathless.

"I wanted to murder Winthrop when I saw the way he was looking at you."

Amanda smiled at his possessiveness. "I think you're overreacting. I told you, we'd just met. I doubt seriously if Bradley was lusting after me."

"Of course he was. Winthrop wanted you. *Any* man would want you," he said while his hands and mouth continued to worship her body. "When I saw you with him and Martha tonight, when I thought you were going to help them take Summer from me..." His voice dropped lower. "They'll never win now—not with you on my side."

Amanda went still. Suddenly the flame inside her fizzled, leaving her feeling cold and sick.

"But I don't want to waste any more time talking about the Winthrops," Michael said, slipping his hand behind her. "I want to make love to you."

He found the zipper at her waist and pulled the tab.

"No!" Amanda pushed him away.

"Amanda, what's wrong?" Michael started to touch her.

"Don't!" She struggled to sit up. Reaching for her dress, she pulled it up over her breasts.

Michael frowned. "What's the matter?"

How could she have been such a fool? She fumbled with the button at her neck, hurriedly fastening it. She'd half convinced herself that she was falling in love with him...and that he cared for her.

He didn't care. He was using her.

Amanda blinked once, twice, fighting to keep the tears at bay.

"Dammit, Amanda, answer me! What in the hell has gotten into you?"

"I've come to my senses. That's what." She smoothed her skirt with as much dignity as possible and made an effort to sit up straight. "Please get dressed, Michael." Her voice was a hoarse whisper.

He looked as though she'd slapped him. He came to his feet in one quick movement. Angrily, he shoved his shirt into his pants and pulled up his zipper.

"A minute ago you were on fire, begging me to make love to you. And now you're trying to tell me you've changed your mind? What kind of game are you playing?" he demanded.

Amanda tipped up her chin. "I'm not playing games. A minute ago I thought it was *me* you wanted."

His brows furrowed. "I did want you. I still do," he said, his confusion evident.

"No. It's not me you want—Amanda Bennett, the woman. You want Dr. Bennett, the child psychologist... someone you think can help you in your custody fight for Summer."

She wanted him to deny it, tell her she was wrong. She could have wept at his lengthy silence, at the hard look in his eyes.

"Is that what you think?" he finally replied.

She tipped her chin a notch higher and met his gaze. "I think Martha Winthrop's suing you for custody of Summer and that you saw me as a weapon against her. That's what that scene tonight was all about, wasn't it?"

"What happened between me and the Winthrops tonight has nothing to do with you. It—"

"Wasn't it?" Amanda demanded.

"Yes," he said, his voice clipped. "Summer's one of the reasons there's bad blood between me and the Winthrops. But you're wrong about the custody suit. Martha hasn't filed one. And I doubt seriously if she will. Oh, she might want Summer, all right, but I don't think she'll want the ugly publicity that a custody battle would generate. She won't want the Winthrop name dragged through the press."

"Suppose you're wrong? Suppose she wants Summer badly enough that she doesn't care about the press?"

"Then we'll go to court and I'll beat her."

"And just how do you plan to do that, Michael? Get me to testify for you? To tell the court what a fine guardian you've been?"

Michael clenched his jaw but didn't answer.

"That is what you planned, isn't it? Isn't that the reason for all the flowers? The romantic dinners?" She bit back a sob. "Isn't that the reason for the big seduction scene tonight?"

"No! Dammit. What happened between us tonight had nothing to do with Summer or the Winthrops." He paced the room, wearing a path across the Aubusson rug.

She wanted to believe him, but she couldn't. She didn't dare allow herself to. She'd been a fool to deceive herself like this. And deceive herself, she had. He didn't care about her; he'd only been using her—just like Adam had used her. She hugged her arms around herself, trying to ease the pain. "I'd like you to leave, Michael."

Michael spun around and crossed over to her. "Amanda, please. Listen to me. Don't do this to us." He eased down beside her. "I—I care for you ... very much. What happened between us tonight was very special to me. I don't want to throw it away. Don't throw *us* away."

Amanda squeezed her eyes shut, wanting desperately to believe him. But she couldn't afford to. She'd been down this road before and sworn not to travel it again. Hadn't she?

She opened her eyes. Squaring her shoulders, she tried to adapt an air of haughtiness. "Since you're so hung up on class, Michael, why not show a little? I've asked you to leave. Now please get out of my house."

Michael's face paled. Slowly he stood. Walking over to the chair, he picked up his jacket. "You know, for a lady who makes her living poking her nose into other people's emotional problems and telling them how to fix things, you haven't done too good of a job of fixing your own."

He hooked the black jacket on his index finger and flung it over his shoulder. "Maybe it's time you took a long hard look at yourself, Dr. Bennett. I don't know what that ex-husband of yours did to you, but maybe someday you're going to stop punishing every man who manages to get close to you for his sins. I just hope when you do, it won't be too late for us."

The next morning Amanda had just finished trying to camouflage the effects of a night that had brought little sleep and far more tears than she'd imagined possible when her doorbell rang. Smoothing the line of her white slacks and nautical top, she walked to the door and opened it.

"Good morning, Amanda," Martha Winthrop said breezily. "May I come in?"

Amanda hesitated a moment. "Martha, this morning's really not a good time for me. I mean, I'm not quite up to company. Could we possibly do this another time?"

"I'm sorry if I'm catching you at a bad time, dear, but this will only take a few minutes. And I'm afraid this simply can't wait."

Although her words were apologetic, her voice lacked sincerity, Amanda thought.

Martha cast a pointed glance at Amanda's neighbor working next door in her garden. "I really do need to speak with you, Amanda, and I think it would be best if this discussion took place in private."

Feeling she had little choice, Amanda opened the door and allowed Martha to enter.

A few minutes later, after serving them coffee, Amanda sat back on the couch. She took a sip from her cup. "Since this is obviously not a social visit, Martha, why don't we skip all the pleasantries and you tell me exactly what it is you need to speak with me about."

"You're very direct, my dear. I like that." Martha set down her cup. "I'll try to be equally direct. Summer Grayson's my granddaughter."

Amanda's stomach tensed, but she remained silent. Taking another sip of coffee, she studied the other woman over the rim of her cup. In her dark navy suit and matching hat, Martha reminded her of a military commander—one who was on a perilous mission.

"Nothing to say, my dear? You don't seem surprised."

Amanda shrugged. "I don't see where it's any of my concern whether Summer Grayson's your granddaughter or not."

"Oh, she's my granddaughter, all right. And I'm glad to see that you're not going to try to deny it. After seeing you with Michael Grayson last night I was afraid you might."

"Get to the point, Martha. What is it you want?"

"Why, your help, of course."

Amanda narrowed her eyes. "My help in what?"

"In ensuring that my granddaughter is given every opportunity to grow up a happy and normal child." Martha toyed with her gloves a moment before lifting her gaze to meet Amanda's. "You see, I know you've been counseling my granddaughter."

Amanda nearly choked on the protest that rushed to her lips, but Martha lifted her hand. "Don't bother to deny it. I know about Summer's behavioral problems and that you've been working with her for nearly three months now. I understand she's progressing quite nicely."

Amanda's fingers tightened on the cup. "I'd be very interested in learning how you managed access to information that's supposed to be confidential."

Martha smiled, but the smile didn't reach her eyes. "This is New Orleans, my dear. I'm a very important person in this town. Most people are only too happy to do small favors for me."

Fuming, Amanda said, "Well, since I'm not from New Orleans, how important you are doesn't mean a thing to me."

"It will, if you're hoping to practice here someday."

Amanda gritted her teeth and wondered what her mother could have possibly found in common with this woman. "If that's supposed to be a threat, I think I'll choose to ignore it."

"That wouldn't be wise."

"Maybe not, but it's my decision. Is that all?"

"No, it isn't. I want my granddaughter, Amanda. And I intend to get custody of her. I'd like you to help me."

"What makes you think I can help you?"

"Because you're her psychologist. And as I'm sure Michael Grayson's already surmised, since you've worked with the child, your testimony would mean a lot in a courtroom."

Amanda fought to remain calm while inside she was seething at the woman's audacity. "Even if I were in a position to help you, which I don't believe I am, what makes you think I would?"

"Because if what your mother told me about you is true, you're a trained psychologist and a good one. You'll do what's best for the child."

"Which means recommending that *you* be appointed her legal guardian?"

"Of course. After all, I *am* her grandmother. And despite the circumstances of her birth, she is a Winthrop. She deserves her heritage. I assure you, I can offer the child a great deal more than that foolish uncle of hers."

"I wouldn't be so sure of that, Martha. Michael Grayson happens to be a fine man," Amanda said, angry at the other woman's disdain. She could easily see where Michael had learned such prejudices if Martha Winthrop were any example of what passed for society in New Orleans. "He loves Summer a great deal and is doing a wonderful job with her."

"Then why does she need a child psychologist?"

"She doesn't—at least, not anymore. She only needed someone to help her work through the pain of losing her mother. And that certainly wasn't Michael's fault."

"No, it wasn't." Martha's lips thinned. "It was Sara's fault for taking my grandchild and running away with her."

Amanda set down her cup. "As I understand it, you weren't all that anxious to welcome her into your home to begin with. Luckily she had a brother who cared enough to stand by her when your son wouldn't."

Some of the starch seemed to go out of the older woman. She sighed, her shoulders sagging slightly. "Yes. That was a dreadful mistake. One I truly regret. But, Bernard, my late husband, wouldn't hear of Phillip marrying the girl."

"Why not?"

"It just didn't seem right for our Phillip to marry the daughter of a former employee."

"Employee? Sara's father worked for you?"

"Why, yes. Didn't Michael tell you? His father worked for our construction company. There was an accident on one of the job sites, a piece of equipment malfunctioned or something, and Michael's father was killed."

Stunned by the revelation, Amanda remained silent as Martha continued.

"The man's wife, poor thing, went completely to pieces. Suffered some kind of breakdown, even tried to kill herself. Bradley and Michael were around the same age . . . and Bradley always did have a tendency to take up with the children of our employees. I guess that's why he knew some of the Grayson kids' friends. Anyway, Bradley said the kids used to call the poor soul Crazy Alice or Mad Alice or something like that because she was always pretending her husband was still alive, that he was coming home. But then, we all know how cruel kids can be sometimes."

Amanda's heart twisted as she remembered the look on Michael's face when Bradley had referred to Crazy Alice. She could easily imagine how difficult those taunts had been for the proud boy Michael would have been.

"Anyway, my Bernard was dead set against Phillip marrying the girl and I wasn't exactly wild about the idea myself."

"Phillip was a grown man. He should have stood up to you and his father."

Martha shook her head. Her eyes misted. "Not my Phillip. He hated confrontation. He was such a quiet boy. He liked music and art. That's what attracted him to the Grayson girl in the first place. I never dreamed I'd lose him and Bernard both so suddenly."

"Is that when you decided you wanted Summer?"

"I've always wanted my grandchild," she said firmly. Martha's eyes flashed and she wiped away any trace of tears. "Sara knew that. That's why she took Summer and ran away. And it's also the reason she would never stay in any one place very long. Because she knew I'd find her and my granddaughter. But she's gone now and Summer's back. I want my grandchild, Amanda. And I mean to have her."

"Michael's her guardian."

"For now. I intend to change that."

Amanda's stomach knotted. "What about Summer? Don't you want what's best for her?"

"Of course I do."

"Then how can you even think of taking her away from Michael? He's the only family she's ever known. It would be heartless to take her away from him."

"Heartless?" she asked, her voice incredulous. "Hardly. Sensible is more like it. When you consider all that I can do for her, it would be foolish to leave her with her uncle."

"But Summer adores him. It'll break her heart."

"Don't be so melodramatic, Amanda. The child will adjust. Besides, I'm not opposed to Summer seeing her uncle—even though he refused me the same privilege."

Fear clawed at Amanda. Fear for Summer. For Michael. "For heaven's sake, we're talking about a child, a flesh-and-blood little girl with feelings. Can't you and Michael work this out instead of fighting over her like she's... like she's some kind of prize in a contest?"

"Since you're the one on such friendly terms with Michael Grayson, why don't you ask him that question yourself? I'm through begging for a chance to know my granddaughter. From now on, I'll do my talking through the courts."

Martha stood. She picked up her bag and her gloves. "I can see from your defense of him, that Michael's already gotten you under his spell. Just remember, my dear, Michael Grayson's a street fighter. He'll do anything and everything to win. And he doesn't care who he uses in order to get what he wants. If I were you, I'd be very careful or you're liable to find yourself tossed out on your pretty little rear when you've outlasted your usefulness."

Seven

If he had any sense, he would forget about her, Michael told himself as he turned the wheel of his car and pulled into the nearly empty parking lot of Saint Margaret's.

But he couldn't. Heaven knew, he'd tried for the past six days. He'd even made an excuse and avoided meeting her after Summer's last session—not that it had done him any good. He'd still been forced to listen to Summer sing Amanda's praises.

Shoving the car door closed, he headed for the school building. Maybe he *had* overreacted, he admitted. He'd certainly been angry at the sight of Amanda with the Winthrops. What a relief it had been to discover he had been wrong and that she hadn't betrayed him.

He drew in a deep breath and released it, remembering the way Amanda had looked at him out of those big brown eyes. She'd made him feel so special, said such sweet, wonderful things to him. And when he'd kissed her and she'd ignited in his arms...

Michael shook his head, trying to blot out the memory of the taste of Amanda's lips, the feel of her soft, silken skin. But he couldn't shake that last image of her eyes filled with pain and accusation, her chin tilted proudly as she'd ordered him to leave.

He'd left there feeling like the lowest form of life.

Michael kicked a rock, his sense of guilt intensifying for not telling her the truth. But he hadn't lied to her when he'd told her he hadn't made love to her because of Summer.

He hadn't.

Of course, he also hadn't told her the real reason he had pursued her in the beginning. Still, he had been honest when he'd said that the potential custody suit had had nothing to do with his making love to her.

It hadn't. What had happened between them hadn't been planned. He'd wanted her simply for herself. And it wasn't just lust. He rubbed the tense muscles at the base of his neck as he strode down the cement walkway toward the school. The problem was, he liked her, and had meant it when he'd told her he cared about her.

And because he had begun to care about her, he was churning inside with guilt. Irritated by this new weakness in himself, Michael yanked open the door.

"Michael!!" Sister Mary Grace stumbled, nearly falling as she came through the door.

Quickly, he reached out a hand to steady her. "Sister, I'm sorry. I didn't see you."

"Obviously," she said, adjusting the deep blue veil of her habit. She resettled the books in her arms. "I guess you're here to pick up Summer."

"Yes."

"I think she's still in Amanda's office." She smiled. "Summer's really done well, hasn't she?"

"Yes, she has."

"And Amanda tells me she won't be needing many more counseling sessions."

"As a matter of fact, today's her last one," Michael informed her, remembering the strained conversation when Amanda had called to advise him.

"You must be very pleased."

But he wasn't, at least not entirely, he realized. Because now he would no longer have any excuse to see Amanda. And after the other night, he doubted if she would agree to see him again on a personal basis.

"I'm glad things worked out so well. I know you were concerned about Summer and didn't like the idea of her seeing a psychologist."

"Yeah, but I was wrong and you were right, Sister. Summer's a different child now because of you. She's much happier than the little girl I brought in here a few months ago. I appreciate everything you've done for her."

"I haven't done anything. The one you should be thanking is Amanda. She's the one responsible for the change in Summer."

"Yeah, I guess she is."

Sister Mary Grace smiled again, her eyes twinkling. Then she glanced at her watch. "Heavens! Look at the time. I have to run or I'm going to be late for evening prayers. Goodbye, Michael." She started down the walkway at a rapid pace, then turned and called back over her shoulder. "Don't forget about the fair next weekend. I expect to see you and Summer both."

"Don't worry, Sister, we'll be there."

Michael entered the school building and walked through the empty halls, now silent except for the ticking of the wall clock. He stepped inside the reception area that had become so familiar to him during the past four months.

Four months. During that time Summer had gone from a quiet, sad-eyed little girl to a happy, smiling one. And it had been because of Amanda.

Sister Mary Grace was right. He did owe Amanda his thanks. And maybe he owed her an apology, too. Michael paused outside Amanda's office.

"But I like talking to you. Why can't I keep coming to see you?" Summer asked.

The door was slightly ajar and Michael peered through the narrow opening at the dark-haired child he'd come to love so dearly and at the woman who stirred not only his blood but some new, unfamiliar feelings of tenderness in him.

"Summer, I explained that to you already. You don't need me anymore. You're doing fine in school now...even in Mrs. Green's class. Aren't you?"

"Yes."

"And we talked about your mother, about her dying. And you realize you don't have anything to feel guilty about. Don't you?"

"Yes."

"You're not having any more bad dreams. Are you?"

"No."

"And we both know you've got your uncle wrapped around your little finger."

Summer giggled.

"So what do you need me for?"

Summer's smile faded. "I need you to be my friend," she said softly.

"Oh, honey." Amanda came from around the desk and knelt down in front of Summer.

Michael swallowed. Amanda looked so gentle, so loving, he thought, much the way she had Saturday night when she'd told him there was nothing common about him.

"I'll always be your friend." She touched Summer's cheek. "Just because I'm not your counselor anymore doesn't mean we'll stop being friends."

"Promise?"

Amanda held up her hand as though taking an oath. "Promise. Girl Scout's honor."

Summer tilted her head to one side. "Now that you're not my counselor anymore, can I call you Amanda the way Sister Mary Grace does?"

"I think Miss Amanda would be better," Michael said, stepping into the room.

Amanda looked up, her expression guarded as she met his eyes. She came to her feet.

"Hi, Uncle Mike." Summer bounded out of her chair and came over to him.

"Hi yourself, Shortstuff." Michael dropped down to the floor and gave Summer a big hug. "Sorry I'm late," he told Amanda as she retreated behind her desk.

"No problem. Summer and I were just saying our good-byes." She shuffled some papers into a folder and closed it. "You do remember that today is Summer's last session?"

Slowly, Michael came to his feet. "I remember." He willed her to look at him, but she continued to avert her gaze. "Maybe we should discuss that. I know we agreed on you working with her until the end of the school term, but it's only been a few months. Maybe we should continue with the counseling until the fall. Of course, I'd be willing to pay you for your services."

"I appreciate the vote of confidence, Michael. But I think you'd be wasting your money. Summer's doing fine. She really doesn't need my help any longer."

"But we're still going to be friends," Summer piped in. "Aren't we, Amanda?"

"Miss Amanda," Michael corrected.

"Aren't we, Miss Amanda?" Summer repeated.

The look she gave Summer was filled with warmth and affection. "That's right," she said softly. "We're going to be friends."

"Then I'd say you're one lucky little girl. Because Miss Amanda's a very special lady. I don't know what we would have done without her."

Amanda looked at him, her eyes questioning as they locked with his.

What was going on behind those deep brown eyes? he wondered. Was she remembering, too? The way it had been between them. The heat. The passion. The overpowering need to be close to one another.

"Come on, Uncle Mike." Summer tugged at his arm. "We need to go or I'm going to be late for Michelle's slumber party."

Amanda's cheeks colored and she looked away.

"All right, sweetheart. Why don't you get your things together while I talk to Miss Amanda for a minute?"

"Okay," Summer said, racing toward the door. "My bag's already packed. I just have to get it from my locker."

Once Summer had left the room, Michael turned to face her. "Amanda."

"Yes?" she replied, but continued to avoid his gaze.

"Amanda, look at me. Please."

She looked at him then, her expression wary, troubled. "What is it you want, Michael?"

He smiled at her, wishing he could ease this tension between them. "To thank you. For everything you've done for Summer . . . for me."

"You're welcome. But Summer deserves most of the credit. She's a terrific little girl and she's worked very hard."

"But she couldn't have done it without you." He paused a moment, then continued. "I meant what I said, Amanda. I don't know what we would have done without you."

"Somehow, I think you'd have managed just fine."

"Do you? I'm not so sure." At the sound of running feet in the hall, Michael glanced at the door. Suddenly he felt nervous. "Look. About what happened the other night—"

"Forget it."

"I don't want to forget it. I owe you an apology and—"

"You don't owe me anything. We both made a mistake. We should never have gone out together in the first place." She began picking up files and placing them in a stack on her desk.

"Dammit, Amanda. Will you stop fidgeting and let me finish?"

Amanda froze. Slowly, she set down the report in her hands. "I do not fidget," she said, tilting her chin slightly.

Michael bit back the urge to smile at her indignant expression. "All right, you don't fidget. But will you at least stay still long enough for me to tell you how sorry I am for the way things turned out the other night?"

She stood stiffly, saying nothing.

"I mean, I said some pretty lousy things about you, about your marriage. I had no right to take my frustrations and anger out on you. I'm truly sorry."

"Apology accepted. Now, if you'll excuse me . . ."

Michael sat on the corner of her desk. "I don't want things to end between us like this, Amanda. Give me a chance to make it up to you. Have dinner with me tonight?"

"I can't," she said quickly. "I have a big exam to study for."

"What about coffee, then? We could grab a cup whenever you take a break. I know a great little place we can go to, an old-fashioned coffeehouse that serves great desserts and the best cappuccino in the city. It's only about ten minutes from your place."

"Michael, this really isn't necessary. I've already accepted your apology. Let's leave it at that."

"I can't leave things the way they are between us, not without at least explaining why I acted the way I did."

"Uncle Mike?" Summer stood at the door, book bag in hand. "I'm ready."

"Be right there, honey." He turned back to Amanda. "Have coffee with me. Give me a chance to explain. If you still don't want to see me after we've talked, I'll leave you alone."

Amanda hesitated.

"Please."

"All right," she said. "Where should I meet you?"

Relief rushed through him. "I'll pick you up."

"No. I'll meet you there—at nine. What's the name of this place?"

"But—"

"Uncle Mike. I'm gonna be late." Summer shifted from one foot to the other. "We have to go."

He glanced from Summer to Amanda. "Okay." He scribbled the name and address on a piece of paper and handed it to her. "I'll see you at nine."

At nine o'clock Amanda stood at the entrance to the coffeehouse and wondered if she had made a mistake in coming. She'd agreed to meet Michael to convince him things were over between them. Yet she'd barely been able to look him in the eye earlier without thinking of what happened or had almost happened between them last Saturday.

Last Saturday. She fought the rush of color climbing her cheeks as she remembered her wanton response to him. Never in her life had she acted so rashly.

And never in her life had any man made her feel so much like a woman.

How was she going to convince him that things were over between them when the mere thought of sitting across from him made her stomach flutter?

She would simply be honest, she told herself. Explain to him that a relationship with him held too many complications, posed too many risks—risks she wasn't willing to take.

Bracing herself, Amanda pushed open the door and stepped inside the coffeehouse. The lights were soft, but not dark. A guitarist strummed gentle folk songs from a seat in the center of the room. Amanda scanned the cluster of tables, searching for the familiar dark head.

Be honest with him, she coached herself silently. Explain that she liked him, was attracted to him, but it would be a mistake for them to become involved any further.

And after she had warned him about Martha, she would leave. Then maybe she would be able to put Michael Grayson and this myriad of feelings he inspired behind her and get on with her life.

Amanda glanced to her right and spotted him seated at a corner table staring into a cup of coffee. He looked tired, she thought, noting the trace of shadows beneath his eyes as she drew near.

She stopped in front of him. "Hello, Michael."

He looked up. "Amanda." He came to his feet at once. "I was afraid you might change your mind." He pulled out a chair for her.

"I considered it," she admitted, sitting down.

"I'm glad you didn't. What can I get you to drink?"

"What are you drinking?"

"Cappuccino. Bavarian chocolate."

"I'll have the same."

A few moments later, Michael placed a steaming mug covered with thick white froth in front of her. "Thanks." Amanda wrapped her hands around the heavy china mug, using the cup as an anchor.

She wanted to run. Away from Michael, away from the way he made her feel. But she couldn't—at least not yet. Not until she'd settled things between them. Leaning forward, she sniffed. "This smells wonderful," she said more calmly than she felt.

"It is. The desserts are great, too. Would you like to try one?" he asked, his voice more anxious than she'd ever heard before. "They've got peanut butter pie, cheesecake, almond croissants..."

Michael didn't generally make small talk; yet, he was doing so now, Amanda realized. Why? Was it possible he was nervous, too? For some reason, the thought helped her to relax. "No, thanks."

He shifted in his seat. "Listen, about those things I said the other night...I really am sorry. I was way out of line."

"You've already apologized. But to be honest, there was a lot of truth in some of the things you said. I'm sure it's part of the reason I got so upset in the first place. Once I had calmed down, I realized that."

He took a swallow of his coffee, then set the cup down. "Don't tell me you analyze yourself, too," he joked, obviously trying to ease the tension between them.

Warmed by the knowledge that this was difficult for him too, she attempted a smile. "Professional hazard, I guess. At any rate, you deserve an explanation. Especially after—" Amanda looked down at her coffee "—after what almost happened."

Michael tipped up her chin, forcing her to meet the warmth of his gaze. "There's nothing to be embarrassed about. What happened between us was wonderful. Seeing you, touching you, was one of the most beautiful experiences of my life. I'm only sorry I ruined it for you."

"You didn't. I mean, it was my fault." Nervous, Amanda picked up her spoon and poked at the peak of foam in her coffee. He made her feel too deeply. He made her want too many things—things that could only lead to heartache. "What I'm trying to say is, that's why I agreed to meet you . . . I wanted to explain why I reacted the way I did."

"You don't have to explain anything. Let's just forget it and start over."

Amanda shook her head. "I can't forget it. And I don't want to start over. I should never have let it get started in the first place. It's over between us, Michael. I don't want to see you anymore."

Michael frowned. Sitting back, he folded his arms across his chest. "You're right. I don't understand. So maybe you'd better explain to me why two people who are obviously attracted to one another, who care about each other, shouldn't be together." He paused. "Unless, of course, I was wrong the other night and you think I'm not good enough for you."

"Oh, for pity's sake. I don't give a hoot about your social or financial standing. Those things have nothing to do with it." Where did she begin? How did she explain the scars and insecurities caused by Adam's deception? "It's not you. It's *me*. *My* past is the problem, not yours."

"Your past?"

"Yes," she whispered. Amanda glanced around. Satisfied they couldn't be heard, she continued. "You know I'd been married before? That I'd had a stepdaughter?"

"Yeah. To some attorney in Boston. A widower. The marriage didn't work out."

"What you don't know was the reason the marriage didn't work." Amanda took a sip of her coffee, allowing the warm chocolaty brew to slide down her throat as she dredged up the painful memories. "Adam married me, but he was never in love with me. He loved someone else."

Michael sat forward. "Listen, you don't have to tell me this."

"Oh, but I do. It's the only way I'll be able to make you understand." She drew a deep breath. "Adam lost his first wife to some kind of rare blood disease. Her death devastated him. I think if it hadn't been for his daughter, he might have died of grief himself. Kimberly was the only thing that kept him going.''

Michael reached out and threaded his fingers through hers, and even though she knew she shouldn't, Amanda drew from his strength.

"But her mother's death affected Kimberly, too. She began having nightmares and problems in school—much like the ones Summer was having. Anyway, Adam brought her to the clinic where I worked and one of my associates began working with her.''

Amanda stared past Michael's shoulder at the painting on the wall, aware of the rich jewel colors yet not really seeing them. She forced herself to go back, to remember. ''I met Adam one day when he came by to pick up his daughter. Kimberly was such a sad little girl, a lot like Summer. She was so filled with grief that she'd kept bottled up inside. And, just like Summer, she was an easy child to love.''

She took another breath and continued. ''Anyway, Adam and I started seeing each other. Naturally, Kimberly and I grew closer because we were spending a lot of time together. The three of us were like a family.'' And she'd hoped to add to that family, until... Amanda swallowed. ''Of course, Adam was grateful for my help with Kimberly. He adored her. He listened to everything she had to say. He was so attentive, so understanding.''

"The perfect father.''

"Yes. At least, I thought so. My own father had always been so busy traveling, attending meetings and diplomatic affairs when I was growing up, I didn't see very much of him. I just couldn't believe how devoted Adam was to his daughter. I didn't think any father could be that caring.''

"Sounds like you admired him,'' Michael said.

Amanda smiled ruefully. ''Yes. I guess I did. At any rate, I fell in love with him. When he asked me to marry him, I was on top of the world. Not only was I getting him, but I was getting Kimberly, too.''

"What happened?''

"We got married. I moved into his home, became a mother to his daughter.'' But she hadn't become Adam's

wife, she added silently. "Things had gotten off to a shaky
start after the wedding. I thought we needed to start somewhere fresh. But instead of finding a new home like I'd
wanted to, Adam convinced me it was better for us to stay
in the home he'd shared with his first wife. He said it would
be better for Kimberly. She felt secure there and he didn't
want to uproot her. Of course, he promised me that we'd
find a new house later when Kimberly could handle the
change."

"But you didn't."

"No," she agreed quietly. "Later, I realized it was Adam
who couldn't bring himself to leave the house—not Kimberly. Of course, redecorating was out of the question.
Everything had to remain just the way it was. The place-
ment of the furniture, his dead wife's portrait in the living
room." Amanda's voice broke. "Her photographs in our
bedroom."

Amanda closed her eyes a moment, recalling what a failure she'd felt in that particular room. "The house was a
shrine to his first wife. You have no idea what that's like—
to be jealous of a dead woman. I guess it was Adam's way
of keeping her alive. I was his wife, but she was always the
woman he loved...the woman he remained faithful to
throughout our marriage."

Michael narrowed his eyes. "What are you saying?"

Her mouth suddenly dry, Amanda struggled past the
lump in her throat. "Adam was impotent," she finally said.
She dropped her gaze, unwilling to meet the pity and questions she knew she would find in his eyes. "He had been
since his first wife's death."

And with the admission, all the old self-doubts returned
in force.

If she'd been more of a woman...

If she'd been able to make him want her...

"But surely before you were married... I mean, didn't the
two of you ever..."

"No, we didn't. It...it wasn't like it is with you and me.
I thought he had waited because he loved me."

"And, of course, he didn't bother to tell you about his problem before you married him." His voice was hard.

"No. And then . . ."

Michael muttered a curse.

Chancing a look at him, Amanda was surprised at the depth of anger burning in his blue eyes. "It wasn't his fault entirely. He simply didn't love me. He was still in love with his first wife."

"Then he should never have married you."

"No, he shouldn't have," Amanda agreed. She met his gaze evenly. "But he wanted a mother for his daughter."

Michael stilled. "Is that what he told you?"

"Eventually. When I threatened to leave him unless he agreed to counseling, he finally admitted that he 'cared for me.'" Amanda tossed Michael's own words back at him. She looked him directly in the eye and wondered if he had any idea how much it had hurt her to hear him say those same words. "He told me he'd made a mistake. That we should never have married. He apologized, and admitted he'd done it for Kimberly—because she needed a mother."

Some emotion flitted across his face, but was gone before Amanda had any chance to guess at what it was. She had no trouble identifying the anger radiating from each line of his body. "And obviously you've decided I'm like him."

"I think you both had similar needs. Adam pretended to be in love with me because he needed a mother for his daughter. You pretended to be interested in me because you saw me as a means to help you retain custody of your niece."

Michael's eyes flashed furiously. He leaned closer and said through gritted teeth, "First off, I never pretended to be interested in you. I *am* interested. I have been from the first moment I saw you in that cramped little school office at Saint Margaret's."

Amanda's heartbeat quickened at his thunderous expression, but she remained silent.

"Second . . ." He ticked off another finger. "I'm not in love with another woman, living or otherwise. And if I were, I wouldn't be here with you.

"And you can take my word for it, Amanda, I'm not impotent. In fact, you came pretty darn close to finding that out for yourself the other night."

Color rushed to her cheeks, but Amanda forced herself to remain firm. She refused to allow herself to be used again. "Are you going to tell me that you wouldn't ask me to help you if there's a custody battle for Summer?"

"Of course, I'd ask you to help me. And if Summer started having problems again, I'd ask for your help then, too. But that doesn't have anything to do with my making love to you. I *want* you. And believe me, it doesn't have a damn thing to do with Summer."

He sounded so angry and self-righteous, she could almost believe him. Or maybe she simply wanted to believe him. And therein lay the danger.

"What do you say, Amanda? Will you give us another chance?"

Amanda shook her head. "I can't, Michael. I'm sorry."

Michael swore. "That ex-husband of yours really did a number on you, didn't he? Wake up and look in the mirror, Amanda. You're a beautiful, sensuous woman. You can turn a guy on by just walking into a room. Hell, just smelling your perfume, remembering how you tasted, the way you felt in my arms, makes me ache for you."

He looked at her so hungrily Amanda felt singed by the intensity of his gaze. Still, she couldn't speak.

"I get hard just at the thought of making love to you."

Amanda squirmed in her seat, grateful that this particular corner of the coffeehouse was nearly empty.

"And judging by your response last Saturday, you're not exactly indifferent to me."

"But it's not what I want. *You're* not what I want. I want safe. And you're not safe, Michael."

"Life's not safe. Every time you walk out of your front door, you take a chance. You don't know whether or not you'll make it back home that night. That you won't be hit by a car or shot by a mugger."

"Those are unavoidable risks. You're not."

A muscle ticked angrily in his cheek. "I wouldn't be so sure of that if I were you. I want you, Amanda. And I don't usually give up on something I want . . . especially when I'm convinced you want the same thing. And you do want me, Amanda, only you're too afraid to take what you want." His voice dropped even lower. "I'm not."

"It doesn't matter. I don't intend to make another mistake. I'm not going to let you or anyone else use me again. You'll have to find someone else to help you fight Martha for Summer."

He clenched his hands into fists. "Have I ever asked you to help me? Have I once said anything about needing you to testify in court?"

"Not yet."

"And I doubt that I will. I told you, Martha Winthrop isn't going to risk having her precious family name dragged through the press and letting the people in this town know she has an illegitimate granddaughter."

Suddenly her own problems faded. Amanda's stomach knotted. She could feel the color drain from her face as she realized he really didn't have any idea how dangerous Martha was. "Don't make the mistake of underestimating her, Michael. She wants Summer and she's determined to get her. I doubt if she cares what the press or anyone else thinks."

Michael frowned; he narrowed his eyes. "You sound like you really believe that."

"I do. Martha came to see me Sunday morning. Somehow she found out I'd been counseling Summer. She asked me to help her."

"What did you tell her?"

"No, of course." Did he even need to ask? "She was very angry. She said she's going to fight you for custody."

Michael slammed his fist against the tabletop, rattling the spoons and china against the Formica. Several heads turned in their direction, but he seemed unaware, his thoughts obviously elsewhere.

"She also told me what happened to your father . . . how he'd been killed while working for her company."

He pinned her with eyes that had turned hard and cold. "What else did she tell you?"

"That your mother ... that she took your father's death very hard."

Michael scoffed. "You don't have to dress it up for my sake, Amanda. She told you my mother was crazy. Didn't she?"

"Michael, don't." Amanda reached out to touch his hand but he pulled away.

"Don't what? Admit the truth? Why not? My mother did have a nervous breakdown when my father died and she never recovered. Did your pal Martha tell you what everyone used to call my mother?"

Amanda's heart twisted at the pain in his voice.

"Crazy Alice. That's what everyone called her. After my father died, she'd just sit on the front porch, day after day and wait. Her eyes were always on the corner street, watching, waiting for my dad to come home. She was so crazy in love with him. She just couldn't accept the fact that he wasn't coming back. That he was dead." There was such hurt and bitterness in his voice. "It didn't even matter that Sara or I were still here, that we needed her. She didn't want to live anymore—not without him."

"I'm sorry," she said, knowing how inadequate the words were, how terrible it must have been for a younger, more vulnerable Michael to see his mother that way.

"Well, your friends the Winthrops weren't sorry. Not even a little bit."

At her puzzled expression, he continued. "It was bad enough my dad was killed working on one of their construction sites, but old man Winthrop said the accident was my father's fault ... that he'd been drinking on the job before he slipped off the girder."

"Oh, Michael. How awful."

"It wasn't true," he said with such bitterness Amanda nearly shrank from him. "Sure, my dad drank a few beers now and then, but never on the job. Winthrop was just covering his own skin. He didn't want any questions raised about the safety of his equipment. He'd gotten some stiff fines the year before when a man had been hurt on the job. The last thing he needed was for my family to file a lawsuit.''

"Did you?" she asked.

"No. My mother wasn't in any condition to do that and I was only sixteen, not old enough to do much."

"But surely you could have contacted a good lawyer—"

"And how many lawyers do you think would have touched a case like that? What lawyer would have been willing to take on people as powerful as the Winthrops?" he snapped. "We didn't have any money. And Winthrop had already warned my mother that any further investigation might hold up the insurance money. And I was afraid to do anything that would draw too much attention to us because of my mother's condition. I didn't want the courts to come in and take Sara and me away from her. I could have handled it, but my mother couldn't have. And neither could Sara."

So much injustice, Amanda thought, her heart aching for Michael. No wonder he harbored so much resentment. But that resentment would destroy him if he wasn't careful. And it didn't make him denying Martha all access to Summer right, either. "So you're meting out your own justice," she said, more to herself than to Michael. "You're keeping Summer from her grandmother to get even with the Winthrops."

"I'm doing what I have to do to protect her from the Winthrops," he corrected.

"Martha said you were a street fighter."

"If you mean, do I fight dirty, the answer's yes. If I have to, I will. What else did she tell you about me?"

"She warned me to be careful. She said you'd use me if I gave you the chance and once I'd outlived my usefulness, you'd toss me aside."

"Do you believe her?"

"I'm not sure. But I do believe you love Summer and that you'd do anything to keep her—including using me."

Eight

Amanda pedaled her bicycle down the street, slowly riding through the quiet neighborhood. She passed house after house with neatly trimmed yards and gardens filled with bright spring flowers. A squirrel scurried up a moss-laden oak, bringing a slight smile to her lips—the first one she'd managed in more than a week.

She lifted her face to the bright May sunshine, and the heat of the morning sun warmed her cheeks. The weather was perfect for the opening of Saint Margaret's school fair, she thought, pumping faster as the street inclined slightly. She really should go to show her support for Gracie and the schoolchildren. Besides, she'd promised Summer she would be there.

Summer.

Amanda chided herself silently as thoughts of the dark-haired little girl filled her head. Wasn't it bad enough that she had started to care for the uncle? How could she have allowed herself to become attached to the child, as well? Would she never learn from her mistakes? There was no place for her in Summer's life—especially not now, not after the way things had turned out between her and Michael.

Irritated, Amanda pedaled faster, trying to outrun the restlessness that seemed to plague her whenever she thought of Michael.

Turning the corner, she braked in front of her own yellow-and-white house. The little cottage was still as cheerful as ever. Bright-covered azaleas and phlox bordered the width of the wooden structure, adding to its charm. But today the sight failed to lighten her mood.

Snap out of it, she told herself. Dismounting her tenspeed, Amanda stored it in the attached garage. She had every reason to be happy. She was on the verge of finishing her studies. She had parents who loved her, and wonderful friends like Gracie. And she had just avoided a very narrow escape where Michael was concerned. What in the world did she have to be gloomy about?

The answer was simple. She missed Michael. She'd ordered him out of her life. But how did she get him out of her heart?

After unlocking the door, Amanda entered the house and walked through to the kitchen. Sighing, she grabbed an apple from the bowl of fruit on the counter and polished it against the leg of her jeans. She took a bite, noisily munching on the sweet, juicy fruit before heading into the den. Taking another bite, she set the apple on the coffee table and plumped up the cushions on the green-and-white couch. Flopping down, Amanda stretched out her legs and crossed them at the ankles.

She cut a glance toward the window. Bright sunshine streamed into the room, reminding her once more just how happy and cheerful she should be and how completely miserable she was.

And it was Michael Grayson's fault.

Michael.

Amanda wanted to scream. She *had* to stop thinking about him. But every time she closed her eyes, Michael was with her again—inside her head, inside her heart—just as he had been almost from the start.

He haunted her. Even after eight full days, she could still see his face, remember the way he'd looked that night—his lean, chiseled features pulled into tight, angry lines, his mouth set and unsmiling.

Amanda squeezed her eyes shut and covered her ears with her hands, but she could still hear Michael's angry voice, his biting words...

"So, it's over. Just like that—" He snapped his fingers in front of her face. Anger radiated from every muscle in his body. "—No discussion. No trying to work things out. You just tell me to get lost...that we're finished. And for what? Because you're too damn scared to take a chance?"

Amanda tilted her chin defiantly. "This has nothing to do with me being afraid."

"The hell it doesn't." His voice was a furious hiss and Amanda was vaguely aware of heads turning around them. "Admit it. I broke through that ice wall you've built around yourself and made you feel again. And it's got you so scared, you can't run away fast enough."

"That's not true."

"No? Then why are you calling it quits between us?"

"I've already explained why."

"Explained? No, Amanda. You haven't explained anything. What you've done is convince yourself that I'm like your ex-husband. You're only too happy to believe anything Martha Winthrop tells you because you're scared silly and have just been looking for any reason to push me away."

Amanda shrugged, striving for nonchalance. "Believe whatever you want."

Michael leaned across the table, bringing his face so close to hers that Amanda could smell the spicy scent of his after-shave. "What I believe is that you're a coward."

Stung by his assessment, Amanda gritted her teeth. "Why? Because I came to my senses and decided not to go to bed with you?" She met his gaze evenly. "I've no doubt you're good, Michael, but sex would have only made things more complicated. And I've already told you, I don't like complications."

Michael pulled back as though she'd slapped him. "Is that how you see me? As a complication? Are you trying to tell me that what was happening between us the other night was just sex?" he demanded. "Is that all it was to you?"

"Isn't that what it was for you?" Amanda shot back, determined not to be intimidated by his outrage.

Turning away, Michael swore. The veins in his neck throbbed angrily as he clenched and unclenched his fists.

When he turned back to face her, his eyes were as hard and cold as steel. The knot in Amanda's stomach tightened.

"It was a lot more than that for me. I thought we had a relationship—one that's emotional as well as physical." He drew a measured breath, then continued. "I wanted us to be able to talk to each other. To go places together. To share things," he finished softly.

His gentleness unnerved her, zapped her anger. Why did he have to make this more difficult? He wanted to use her, she told herself, marshaling her defenses. "How can you say that after what almost happened between us? After... after the things you said a few minutes ago?"

"After what? Admitting that you turn me on?"

Her throat tight, unable to speak, Amanda nodded.

"Why not? It's true. I wanted you last night. I still want you," he said, his voice low, husky. "I want to take you to bed, to explore every inch of you with my mouth, with my hands, until I know your body as well as I know my own. I want to lie with you naked, bury myself deep inside you."

Amanda's pulse grew frantic.

"I want to make love to you for hours...slow and easy until we're both desperate with need, then fast and hard because neither of us can wait a moment longer. And then I want to start all over again and not stop until we're both so weak neither one of us can lift our heads."

Breathless, Amanda's heart raced at the provocative images his words created. She gripped the edge of the table unable to do anything more than stare at him.

"But I'm not interested in meaningless sex, Amanda. I never have been."

He pinned her with his gaze and Amanda felt as though his blue eyes could see through the facade she'd tried so hard to erect and into her wanton soul.

"But then, maybe that's what you want," he continued. "Empty sex. Maybe that's your idea of a relationship..."

He made it sound so ugly, so cold. The warm feeling his erotic expounding had caused withered, leaving her chilled, hollow.

"Because you sure as hell don't have a clue about what a real relationship is or what it takes to make one work."

Stung, she snapped, "And I suppose you do?"

"Yeah, I do," he said arrogantly. "At least I have a lot better idea of what it takes than you do."

She shot him her haughtiest look, the one that had successfully banished many an unwanted suitor.

It didn't faze Michael.

"I know it takes a lot of guts to put your feelings on the line, to leave yourself open, to risk being hurt." He gave a short, mirthless laugh that chilled Amanda even more. "And you know what's so ironic?"

"No doubt you're going to tell me," she said, trying for sarcasm but falling short.

"I asked you to meet me here so I could apologize. I thought I'd overreacted the other night when I accused you of being afraid. I wanted to tell you that I was wrong.

"I told myself, here's a woman who's chucked everything, who's picked up the pieces of her life and started over. But you weren't starting over. Were you, Amanda?"

She didn't even attempt to answer him.

"You were running," he said, not bothering to hide his scorn. "And now you're running again—only this time, you're not running from an ex-husband or unhappy memories. Hell, you're not even running from me. You're running from yourself. And the sad part about it is, you don't even know it."

She'd had enough. Pushing back her chair, Amanda stood. "Thank you, Dr. Grayson. Now, if you've finished your amateur analysis, I'm leaving."

Michael's hand flashed out and caught her wrist before she could take a step. Amanda looked down at her imprisoned wrist, locked in his powerful grasp. She brought her gaze back up to his angry face.

"Someday you're going to get tired of running," he told her, his voice low, dangerous. "I only hope when you do, it won't be too late for us."

Amanda shook her head, trying to clear away the memory, but Michael's words continued to echo in her mind.

Had he been right? she asked herself for the dozenth time. Had she been running from herself and her feelings? True, she hadn't wanted the emotional risk a relationship with him represented. But had she deluded herself into believing if she shut him out of her life that her heart would be safe?

Had she succeeded? Or was it already too late?

The telephone rang, saving her from searching for answers that wouldn't come. Sitting up, she swung her legs to the floor. The shrill sound continued to pierce the quiet as Amanda walked over to the table and picked up the receiver. "Hello?" she answered in the middle of the third ring.

"Miss Amanda?"

Amanda knitted her brows. "Summer? Summer, is that you?"

"Yes," Summer returned breathlessly, the relief in her voice evident. "I was afraid I had the wrong number. I asked information for your phone number, but it didn't sound like you at first."

"Summer, honey, is something wrong?" Amanda asked, beginning to feel worried.

"It's Uncle Mike."

Amanda froze. Suddenly her legs grew weak. "Has something happened to your uncle?" she asked, fighting to keep the panic from her voice.

"No. He's all right, it's just that...that he's going to ruin everything."

"Ruin everything? Honey, what are you talking about? What's going to be ruined?"

"Everything," Summer declared, her voice breaking on a sob. "Please, will you come help us?"

"Help with what?"

Summer mumbled something, but the words were drowned out by what sounded like a loud crash.

"Summer, what was that noise?" Amanda demanded.

"Please say you'll come, Miss Amanda. You said you were my friend and Sister Mary Grace said friends help each other. Will you help me?"

"Help with what?" There was another crash and Amanda was sure this time she heard glass breaking. "Summer, what's going on?"

"Uh-oh. I gotta go. Please hurry. We need you. Bye."

"Summer, wait—"

But it was too late, the dial tone was already buzzing in Amanda's ear.

Amanda stood for a moment, looking at the receiver she held in her hand. She depressed the button and punched out the digits for Information.

Amanda jotted down Michael's phone number and address. Picking up the receiver again, she punched out Michael's number.

The line was busy.

She dialed again. Again, she got a busy signal.

Please come. We need you. Summer's pitiful voice kept playing over and over in her head.

Amanda started to dial a third time, but hung up the phone instead.

She was probably making a mistake by going. Only a fool would risk becoming more involved with either Grayson, she told herself.

Evidently, she was a fool.

Grabbing her purse and car keys, she rushed out of the door, ignoring common sense and following her heart.

Twenty minutes later when Summer opened the door and threw herself into Amanda's arms, Amanda was glad her heart had won.

"I knew you'd come," Summer said, clinging to her.

Amanda swallowed, moved by the little girl's faith in her. After a moment she held Summer at arm's length and stood. "Now suppose you tell me what's wrong?"

"It's the school fair," she said, her green eyes filling with tears.

"The school fair?" Amanda asked, confused.

Summer hiccuped. "My class is supposed to bring cupcakes to sell . . ."

Amanda looked around the room and sniffed, wrinkling her nose at the scent of burning cake. "Cupcakes? That's the emergency?"

Summer nodded. "Only, Uncle Mike doesn't know how to bake."

Amanda didn't know whether to be angry or relieved.

"He wanted to buy them, but they have to be homemade. So, he's been trying to bake them . . ."

The smell seemed to grow stronger and Amanda pressed her finger to her nose as it started to sting a little.

"And we're supposed to have them at the school before three o'clock, but—"

"Ouch!" Michael's angry shout came from the next room and was followed by a loud crash. What sounded like metal hit the floor with a bang. A thud came next and was followed by another muttered curse.

"Come on," Amanda said, grabbing Summer's hand. "We'd better get in there before he kills himself *and* burns the house down."

Summer led the way to the kitchen. When she pushed open the door, the smell of burning cupcakes slapped Amanda in the face. She blinked, her eyes smarting. She waved her hand back and forth in front of her face in an effort to ease the odor.

The room was in chaos. A trail of flour covered the counter, ending in a heap of broken eggs, their yellow yolks running down the side of the cabinet. Mixing bowls and measuring cups covered in chocolate cake batter lay strewn across the counter like drunken soldiers. An electric mixer rested on its side, the beaters looking battle worn and weary.

Summer coughed and waved frantically in front of her face. "Uncle Mike, Miss Amanda's here. She's going to help us."

Michael spun around, holding a pan of charred cupcakes in one hand with a bright yellow oven mitt.

With an apron tied haphazardly around his waist, smudges of flour on his face and chocolate cake batter splattered across his T-shirt, on his forehead and in his hair, he was the most wonderful sight she'd ever seen.

And she loved him.

Unnerved by the realization, Amanda squeezed her eyes shut for a moment. Despite all her reservations and her determination not to fall in love with him, he'd somehow managed to slip past her guard and find his way into her heart.

Opening her eyes, she looked at him and wondered if he already knew what she'd just come to realize.

He squinted his eyes against the smoke billowing from the oven and the pan he was holding, and peered in her direction. "What are you doing here?" he asked, his voice guarded.

"Summer called me and said you needed help." She cut a glance to the burned cupcakes he was holding. "And from the looks of things, she was right."

"Nothing we can't handle," he began, squaring his jaw like an indignant child. "We're doing just fi— Ouch!" Michael dropped the pan to the floor and crisp, black cupcakes flew in all directions. He jumped back, cracking his head on the upper oven door.

"Uncle Mike!"

"Michael!"

Summer and Amanda rushed to his side.

He cursed as he rubbed his head with one hand. Flinging off the oven mitt, he stuck his burned fingers into his mouth.

"Be still and let me look at your head," Amanda ordered.

He grimaced as she examined the small knot forming on his forehead.

"Is he all right?" Summer asked anxiously.

"Oh, I think he'll live," Amanda told her, sidestepping one of the smoldering cupcakes. "But I'm not too sure about those cupcakes."

"Funny, Amanda. Real funny," he said.

Amanda bit back a smile. "Summer, do you think you can find me an ice pack?"

"There's one in the bathroom."

"Can you get it for me?"

Summer went running out of the room.

"What do you need an ice pack for?"

"For that hard head of yours." Taking him by the arm, she led him to the sink and turned on the cold water. She stuck his burned fingers under the faucet.

He pulled his hand away.

"You're supposed to put butter on a burn," he complained, obviously disgruntled.

Amanda stuck his hand under the water again. "Not true, and not if you want to stop it from blistering. Stay put until I get a bowl of ice for your hand."

Muttering, Michael turned his back to her and did as he was told.

When Summer returned with the ice pack, Amanda had him seated in a recliner in the living room, his hand immersed in the bowl of ice that rested in his lap. After filling the ice pack, she placed it on his forehead.

"Thanks," he muttered.

"Feeling better?"

"I never felt bad in the first place."

Amanda arched one brow. "No? Could have fooled me. You look like you've been in heavy combat."

When he looked up at her, she was smiling. And despite himself, Michael found himself smiling back. "Yeah, I guess I do look a little battle worn," he admitted.

"A little?"

"All right. A lot." Michael grinned, enjoying her teasing. "But I never claimed to be any good at baking. And that recipe didn't turn out the way it was supposed to."

"So I noticed."

"Uncle Mike," Summer said, bringing in a tray of charred cupcakes. "I don't think these are right, either." She poked at one of the cakes with her finger and the top caved in.

"I followed the directions," he insisted, feeling a bit defensive with both Summer and Amanda looking at him. He'd never baked cupcakes before—only eaten them. But he'd tried darn hard to bake these because it seemed so important to Summer. "I did. I even improved on the recipe."

Amanda looked down at the blackened cupcakes then back up at him. "This is improved?"

"He found some shortcuts," Summer explained.

Michael smiled, proud of his ingenuity. "Instead of spending all that time softening the butter before mixing it with the sugar, I went ahead and melted it."

"And we put in extra chocolate squares so it would taste real chocolaty," Summer added.

Amanda picked up one of the cupcakes, examining where the batter had mushroomed over the top of the paper cup before burning. "I guess you decided to make them extra large, too."

Michael's smile slipped a little as he looked at the pitiful results of his morning's work. "I filled them up with batter just like you're supposed to. Something must be wrong with the oven."

"Of course, the oven," Amanda said solemnly, her lips twitching at the corners.

Summer looked at the cupcakes. "They don't look like the ones Michelle's mom made." Leaning forward, she sniffed at the cupcakes and crinkled her nose. "And they don't smell like Mrs. Darcy's, either."

"I know," Michael said.

Summer turned to Amanda, her shoulders drooped. "I said I'd bring chocolate cupcakes to the fair."

"It's all right, honey," Amanda soothed.

"Do you know how to make cupcakes like Mrs. Darcy's?" she asked, her expression filled with hope.

Amanda smoothed Summer's bangs away from her face. "I don't know if mine will taste as good as Mrs. Darcy's, but I think I can come up with something passable."

"You can bake?" Michael asked.

"You don't have to sound so surprised."

"I'm not. It's just that I hadn't envisioned you spending much time in the kitchen."

"I don't usually have much reason to. And, I admit, I'm not nearly as ambitious as you are. I use a cake mix."

"Does that mean you'll make some cupcakes for me to take to the fair?" Summer asked.

"If your uncle doesn't have any objections." She cut a glance toward him, her eyes questioning.

He shrugged. "It's okay with me." Michael paused, remembering how things had ended between them the previous week. Was that the only reason she'd come? To help Summer? "Sure you want to do this? I wouldn't want you to feel like you were being used."

He heard the tiny catch in her breath, saw the flash in her eyes before she looked away. "I don't."

"Amanda's my friend, Uncle Mike." Summer took hold of her hand. "That's why she came."

"What about us, Amanda? Are we friends, too?" Michael asked.

She shifted as though uncomfortable under his scrutiny. "We can be, if you want us to be," she returned, her voice serious, her eyes questioning.

He wanted a great deal more than simple friendship from Amanda. And it had nothing to do with Summer. He'd discovered that much two days ago when he realized he would no longer need her as his wife to ensure Summer remained in his custody.

And if the flush staining her neck and cheeks as she and Summer headed for the kitchen was anything to go by, she wanted a lot more than friendship, too.

Leaning back in his chair, Michael smiled. He'd been waiting for the right moment to approach her again. But, thanks to Summer, his waiting was over.

His sweet little minx of a niece had given him a second chance with Amanda. And this time, he was going to do his best not to blow it.

Michael stood at the doorway and watched Amanda move around his kitchen, laughing and working with Summer. He'd been pleased to see how quickly she'd taken over, directing him and Summer easily until she had restored the place to order.

He smiled, enjoying the sight of her face flushed with excitement. With her long blond hair caught up in a ponytail and one of his aprons wrapped around her tiny waist, she was a far cry from the Boston socialite or the cool Dr. Amanda Bennett he'd first met. She looked like a woman, a beautiful, contented woman.

And he wanted her to be his.

"Uncle Mike." Summer spotted him standing at the door. "Come see," she said excitedly, motioning for him to enter.

He walked into the room and moved beside his niece.

"Don't they look great?" Summer asked as she held up a tray of beautifully frosted chocolate cupcakes.

"Sure do." He scooped a fingerful of frosting off the top of one and stuck it in his mouth. "Hmm. Taste good, too. How about a sample?"

Summer looked at Amanda. "Can he have one?"

"Oh, I think we can spare one," Amanda said, smiling. She turned on the dishwasher, then walked across the kitchen and moved next to Summer. "But no more for you, missy," She tapped the tip of Summer's nose. "You've already had two."

"Two?" Michael arched his brow. Taking one of the cupcakes from Summer's tray, he peeled back the paper.

"I was the tester and I helped frost them, too," Summer explained proudly.

"Tester, huh?" Michael bit into the cupcake, finishing off the sweet chocolate cake in two bites. He swallowed. "If you guys hadn't banned me from the kitchen, I'd have tested them for you." He licked the chocolate frosting and crumbs from his fingertips. "That was really good."

"And they taste even better than Mrs. Darcy's," Summer added, her eyes shining.

Michael licked the last of the chocolate frosting from his lips. "That good, huh? Maybe I should test another one just to make sure."

He reached for a second cupcake, but Amanda slapped his hand away and laughed. "I don't think that'll be necessary," she said, smiling at him. "Summer, you'd better box these up now or they may not make it to the fair."

"Okay." Summer hurried over to the table to pack up her precious cupcakes.

"Don't you want to know if I think your cupcakes taste as good as Mrs. Darcy's?" Michael teased.

"Not really." She moved over to the counter and picked up a large mixing bowl. Standing on tiptoe, she reached up to store it in the cabinet.

"Let me get that," Michael said, moving behind her. He'd only meant to help, but then his legs accidentally touched the back of her legs and his fingers brushed hers as they both slid the bowl onto the shelf.

All the lightness and teasing of a few moments ago deserted him instantly. And the memories came flooding back. The way she'd felt in his arms. The sweet taste of her lips...

Amanda snatched her hand away. "Thanks," she said, her voice a shaky whisper.

His hands drifted down and settled on either side of the counter, trapping her within the circle of his arms.

Slowly, she turned to face him, her eyes dark and shiny as they met his. Michael leaned closer. "Amanda..."

"All finished," Summer said.

Michael shook his head to clear it, then dropped his hands to his sides.

Grinning from ear to ear, Summer carried the large box of cupcakes over to them. "Can we go now?"

"Heavens, look at the time," Amanda said, glancing at her wristwatch. "It's after two. You two had better get going if you want to get these to the fair by three."

"We've got plenty of time," Michael assured her. "I've already showered and changed. And you sent Summer up to change when she finished with the frosting, remember?"

He took the box from Summer and placed it on the counter, then turned back to his niece. "Summer, don't you have something you want to say to Amanda?"

"Thank you," Summer said.

"You're welcome."

Summer wrapped her arms around Amanda's waist and hugged her. "I wish you could stay here with us all the time. I love you."

Dropping to her knees, Amanda hugged Summer close. She blinked, her eyes glistening with tears as she whispered, "I love you, too."

Michael swallowed, moved by the affection between the child he'd come to love and the woman who had stolen his heart. This is how it would be if they were a family, he thought. The three of them—Summer, Amanda and him.

Summer pulled back from Amanda. "Will you come with us to the fair?"

"Oh, honey, I don't think so." At Summer's crestfallen expression, she added, "But I'm planning to go later this afternoon. Maybe I'll see you there."

But if that skittish look in her eyes meant anything, she would be careful to avoid him. "Have you already made other plans?" Michael asked as casually as he could.

"No."

"Then why not come with us?"

"I couldn't. You're ready to go now and look at the way I'm dressed," she protested.

Michael ran his gaze over her, taking in the white oxford shirt with its sleeves rolled up past her elbows and tucked into the worn, faded jeans that molded her trim hips and long legs. He smiled at the sight of the sensible white tennis shoes before moving back up to her face. Flawless and free of makeup, her skin looked like ivory silk, her eyes the color of dark topaz. "You look beautiful to me." And she did. Beautiful on the inside and outside.

"Please come with us." Summer tugged at her hand.

Amanda hesitated and Michael sensed her indecision. He wanted her with him...with them. The three of them belonged together. He'd been a fool to even think he could have walked away from her. He couldn't. And he wasn't going to let her walk away from him—not without a fight. "I'd like you to come, too, Amanda. Will you?"

"All right," she said, giving in. "But I'm at least going to change clothes. I'm not going anywhere with chocolate cake batter smeared all over me."

"Okay," Michael agreed. He picked up the box of cupcakes. "We'll stop by your place on the way to the fair."

Summer practically danced to the door. "We're going to have so much fun," she said excitedly. "We'll be just like a real family."

And someday they would be a real family, Michael promised himself as he closed the door. The three of them belonged together. And he was going to find a way to convince Amanda of that. He simply had to.

He only hoped he could do it before Martha filled Amanda's head with any more doubts about him.

Nine

———

"Let's go again." Summer tugged on Michael's hand, urging him back in line for the Ferris wheel.

"Why don't we try something that stays on the ground?" Michael asked, digging in his heels.

Amanda laughed. "Chicken."

"Not chicken," he countered. "Just not wild about heights. Besides, all that spinning around can't be good for the digestion."

"Is that why you turned such a delightful shade of green when we reached the top?" Amanda teased. "I thought it was all that stuff you piled on your hot dogs."

"Look who's talking. A woman who thinks a hot dog is supposed to be just bread and meat." He smiled at her. "Admit it. Didn't it taste better my way?"

"Yes," Amanda agreed, sighing. But then everything tasted better, looked better, *was* better when she shared it with Michael.

Amanda hugged the stuffed white bear Michael had won for her at the ringtoss, feeling happier than she had in years.

Glancing around her, she took in the spinning wheel, the bright colored balloons, the families moving about. She listened to the laughter and squeals of the children, the reedy sound of music coming from the calliope that she'd always associated with a carnival.

She really *was* happy, she admitted. And for the first time in a long while, she felt as though she belonged. Not just to the city and community, but with the man and child beside her.

As they neared one of the red-and-white striped concession stands, Amanda took a deep breath and inhaled the tantalizing scent of fresh popcorn.

"Want some?" Michael asked, stopping in front of the booth.

Amanda's mouth watered, but she shook her head. "I don't know where I'd put it. I'm still stuffed from the hot dogs."

"I'm not," Summer told them. "And I love popcorn."

"I'm beginning to think you love food, period," Michael told her. After he paid the attendant, he handed the bag of buttered popcorn to Summer.

A few minutes later Summer tossed the empty bag into the trash can and licked the last of the salt from her fingers. Looking up at her uncle, she asked, "Can we go on another ride now?"

"Sure." Michael ruffled Summer's hair, then led them through the chattering crowd back toward the amusement rides. "But I meant what I said—nothing that requires us leaving the ground. How about the carousel?"

Amanda's gaze sought his. Her breath caught at the heat in his eyes and she knew he was remembering their dinner in the Carousel Pavilion, too.

"The carousel's for babies," Summer informed them, breaking the charged moment. "What about the bumper cars?"

"Sorry, Shortstuff. The sign says you have to be twelve. You've still got a few years to go."

Amanda laughed at Summer's crestfallen expression. "Don't worry. It'll be here before you know it."

Sighing dramatically, Summer rolled her big green eyes. "That's what everyone says."

"Then maybe everyone's right," Michael told her, chucking her under the chin.

They passed a row of booths offering an assortment of prizes. "How about some games?" Amanda suggested. "Maybe we can win another stuffed animal."

Several quarters and one stuffed tiger later, Summer was obviously longing for more adventure. Amanda was considering taking the little girl to ride the Ferris wheel without Michael when suddenly Summer stopped. She spun around to face them, her eyes bright with excitement. "What about the haunted house?"

Amanda jerked to attention and stared at the large tunnel-like structure with tracks running through it. "You don't want to go in there," she said, making a face. "Those things aren't any fun."

"Oh, but it is," Summer assured her. "Michelle said it's great. She's already gone three times."

"It's dark and spooky," Amanda argued.

Summer grinned. "I know."

Amanda's stomach sank. "Suppose you got scared? You might even have nightmares later." Nervous, Amanda hugged the small stuffed bear with both arms.

"I won't. I promise, Miss Amanda. Besides, everybody knows it's only make-believe. There aren't *really* any such things as ghosts or monsters. Are there, Uncle Mike?"

"Nope. They're just make-believe."

But knowing that didn't stop Amanda's heart from sticking in her throat at the thought of going inside.

"And I'm not afraid of the dark," Summer assured Amanda. "Am I, Uncle Mike?"

"No, you're not. You're a very brave girl." Michael turned his attention to Amanda. "What about you, Amanda? Are you a brave girl, too? Or are you afraid of the dark?"

Amanda shrugged. "Maybe a little."

But she was lying through her teeth. She hated the dark. Always had. That's the reason she still kept a night-light burning in her bedroom. She also wasn't particularly fond of having things jump out at her in the dark. Amanda shuddered. She'd never understood why anyone would ever allow themselves to willingly be scared witless.

"If you'd rather not go, it's all right," Michael said. "I can take Summer, or we can all go on the Ferris wheel again instead."

Amanda's chest tightened. Michael was petrified of the Ferris wheel. His face had gone white when they'd reached the top and he had held on to the safety bar as though his life had depended on it. Yet, he was willing to go again to spare her the haunted house.

"You don't have to be afraid," Summer soothed. "It really is just make-believe. Those aren't really ghosts and skeletons in the haunted house—just some of the bigger school kids dressed up."

Amanda smiled. "I know."

"And Uncle Mike will protect you. Won't you, Uncle Mike?"

"That's right." His eyes were dark and serious as they met Amanda's. "Trust me, Amanda. I won't let anything hurt you. I promise."

Amanda swallowed, hoping he wasn't only talking about the haunted house.

"What do you say?" Michael asked softly. "Are you willing to take a chance?"

He made her want to take chances, to take risks, to be daring. He made her want to believe in dreams again, in happily-ever-afters and till-death-do-us-parts. He made her want to risk loving again. "Yes," she whispered. But it wasn't the carnival ride she'd just agreed to take a chance on—it was Michael.

Squealing, Summer grabbed one of Amanda's hands. "Let's get in line."

Smiling, Michael laced his fingers with Amanda's and then the three of them raced toward the haunted house.

Summer spotted her friend Michelle and darted over to exchange stories. Ten minutes later when they neared the front of the line, the two girls raced back to Amanda and Michael.

"Michelle's mom doesn't want to go through again. Can I ride in the car with her?" Summer asked.

"Please, Mr. Grayson?" Michelle pleaded.

"Sure you won't be afraid by yourself?" Michael asked Summer.

"Not if I know you and Miss Amanda are in the car behind us."

"Don't worry, Mr. Grayson. I'll look out for her," Michelle informed him, drawing herself up to her full height of less than four feet.

"All right. You girls go ahead. Amanda and I will be in the car right behind you."

Squealing, the two youngsters piled into the small yellow car and the attendant sent it on its way.

The next car stopped in front of them. "Ready?" Michael asked.

"Ready." Amanda got in and Michael slipped into the seat beside her. The attendant pulled the safety bar closed and with a slight jerking motion, the car started down the track. As they neared the mouth of the dark tunnel, Amanda swallowed. Adrenaline rushed through her and she gripped the rail that rested in front of her.

Michael eased his arm around her shoulders. "Relax," he said, pulling her close.

But relaxing was impossible. As they entered the tunnel, Amanda blinked. Once. Twice. She tried to adjust her eyes to the sudden darkness.

A skeleton shot out in front of them.

Amanda screamed and launched herself into Michael's arms. She buried her head against his chest.

"Hey, it's okay," he soothed. Gathering her in his arms, he began stroking her back. "You don't have to be afraid. I've got you."

"I—I'm sorry." She lifted her head and attempted to pull back, but Michael pressed her head back down against his chest.

His arms tightened around her. "Don't apologize. I certainly don't mind." The timbre of his voice sent tremors down her spine.

The car moved along at a snail's pace, but Amanda kept her eyes firmly shut despite the eerie moans and groans, the screams around them.

Michael continued to run his fingers up and down her spine in slow, soothing strokes. His lips brushed her hair. Eventually she relaxed against him, her fear slipping away.

Conscious only of Michael, Amanda snuggled closer as the delicious sensations his touch was causing continued to build. She took a deep breath, hoping to slow her quickening pulse. Instead, she inhaled the earthy scent of leather and soap that she'd come to associate with Michael and her heart raced even faster.

Amanda burrowed closer, feeling safe, secure.

At the sound of a flapping noise, she eased open one eye to chance a peek. A loud shrill pierced the air as a batlike creature swooped down near her head. Amanda screamed. She clutched at Michael.

"Hey, it's all right. It's all right," he murmured. "I've got you," he told her as the car inched forward, leaving the bats behind.

"I hate bats," she said, unable to stop her hands or her voice from shaking.

"They're not real, Amanda. Just bits of painted cardboard and wire."

"I know. But I can't help remembering all those old vampire movies. They always did frighten me." Amanda shuddered again involuntarily.

Michael rubbed her arms gently.

"I'm sorry. I know I'm being foolish."

Michael tilted her chin up with his thumb and forefinger and she stared into his warm blue eyes. "There's nothing wrong with admitting our fears. We all have them. Besides," he said, grinning, his teeth gleaming white and even in the darkness, "if there really was a Count Dracula, I don't think I could blame him if he wanted to bite *your* neck." His fingertips moved along her cheek and down her throat. "It's such a beautiful neck."

Suddenly Amanda forgot about her fear of the dark and the bats. She forgot about the haunted house. She forgot about the eerie sounds and the distant screams of people inside the other cars.

She forgot about everything but the feel of Michael's arms wrapped loosely around her, the sensation of his fingers moving lazily up and down the arc of her neck, along the tip of her ear. She splayed her hands against his chest and felt the rapid thudding of his heart beneath her fingertips.

"But if our old friend Dracula had any sense at all, it wouldn't be just your neck that he'd want to taste."

Hearing the deep, husky tone of his voice, Amanda's own throat felt suddenly tight. She peered up at him. Surrounded by darkness, his face was all that filled her vision. "It wouldn't?" she asked, unable to tear her eyes away from the firm line of his jaw, his full sensuous mouth.

"No." He drew his finger down her cheek and slowly across her mouth. "If he had any sense, he'd want to taste these lips."

"Michael," she whispered, arching her body toward him, wanting, needing his kiss, his love.

He needed no further invitation.

His mouth closed over hers, gently tasting, teasing. Amanda parted her lips, welcoming his tongue. She traced his lips with her own tongue and Michael groaned, sending a shiver of excitement through her.

When he took possession of her mouth a second time, his lips were harder, hungrier, hotter. Amanda felt as though she were on a roller coaster, zipping faster and faster along unsteady tracks toward some dangerously high cliff.

She clung to him. Her fingers curled into tight fists, crumpling his shirt, before she slid her arms up and encircled his neck.

Michael deepened the kiss. Then suddenly, without warning, she found herself plunging downward at breakneck speed. But she no longer cared. All that mattered was that they were together, locked in one another's arms.

When the car slammed through the swinging doors out into the waning sunlight, Amanda opened her eyes. Her breath came in short, quick gasps and it took a moment before she realized where she was. Once she did, she started to move away, but Michael held her beside him for a second longer before easing his hold and helping her out of the car.

"Wasn't that fun?" Summer asked, racing over to them with her friend, Michelle.

"I certainly enjoyed myself. What about you, Amanda?" His eyes caressed her face.

"Yes," she replied breathlessly, her legs still weak. Dear Lord, how could she have lost control that way? she wondered as she retrieved her stuffed bear from the floor of the car.

"Were you scared?" Summer asked her.

"A little," she admitted. She smoothed back her hair with unsteady fingers. But it wasn't the dark that had shaken her. It was Michael. Being in his arms was more dangerous and exciting than the wildest of rides.

"But Uncle Mike took care of you," Summer said proudly.

"Yes."

"I told you he would."

"Yes, you did." But no one had warned her that Michael would kiss her senseless and turn her life upside down.

"Since Miss Amanda's not afraid anymore, can we ride it again?" Summer asked her uncle.

"Please, Mr. Grayson." Michelle dragged out the words, pleading.

Michael turned to Amanda and smiled. "What do you say? Want to try it again?" Amanda caught the note of amusement in his voice and the hungry gleam in his eye.

Did he have any idea how affected she'd been by that kiss? She couldn't go through that again—not here. A school fair was no place for the kind of kiss they had just shared. "Why don't you and the girls go ahead? I'm a little thirsty. I think I'll get something to drink."

"You know, my throat feels a little dry, too. I think I'll go with you." Michael dug in his pocket and pulled out some bills. He handed them to Summer. "You and Michelle go ahead. Amanda and I will wait for you over by the lemonade stand." He pointed to the yellow-and-white-striped booth. "Okay?"

"Okay," they said in unison before running back to the line.

"You should have gone with them," Amanda chided. "Suppose Summer gets scared or—"

Michael placed his index finger to her lips. "Summer will be fine. Besides, you're the one who looks shaken."

She started to object, but Michael was already reaching for her hand. "Come on," he said, lacing his fingers through hers. "Right now, I could use something cool. Let's go get that lemonade."

Several lemonades and a few hours later, Amanda came down the stairs from Summer's bedroom. "Did she give you any trouble?" Michael asked, noting the troubled look in her eyes.

Amanda shook her head. "Once I got her into bed, she went right to sleep."

"Good. She's had a pretty full day." He led her into the living room and they sat down on the couch. "So have you," he said, tucking a stray hair behind her ear. He didn't know why Amanda had decided to stop running from him, he only knew that he was glad that she had. He allowed his finger the pleasure of trailing down her neck. She had the softest, most beautiful skin, he thought. He was beginning to think he could spend a lifetime touching, exploring that skin, and it still wouldn't be long enough.

Amanda caught his hand and stilled it. She looked up at him, her expression somber. "Michael, you haven't mentioned anything about Martha Winthrop. Have you heard any more from her or her attorney?"

Michael tensed. Would they never get beyond that? Sighing, he pulled back his hand. "The last time her name came up you and I ended up in a fight and I almost lost you." Even now Amanda's accusations and the pain he had caused her bothered him. He'd been afraid he'd lost her for good. "I think it would be better if we didn't discuss Martha Winthrop at all from now on."

"You're probably right. But I have to know. Has she sued you for custody?"

She hadn't—at least, not yet. But from what Dave had told him, the papers were being prepared. What would Amanda say if she knew that? Would she run away from him again? Convince herself he was using her?

And what chance would he have of convincing her otherwise? Especially, when in the beginning he had planned to do just that? The less she knew, the better, he decided—at least, for now. He wouldn't risk losing her again. "Forget about Martha Winthrop. She's my problem, Amanda. Not yours."

"I realize that, but—"

"But nothing." He'd been given a second chance with Amanda and he refused to let Martha ruin things. "I'll deal with Martha if and when the time comes. You don't need to worry about her."

"But I am worried and you should be, too. Summer's trying to find her."

Michael froze. His heart stopped a moment. Narrowing his eyes, he studied Amanda. She wouldn't have told Summer that Martha was her grandmother. She couldn't possibly betray him that way, he told himself. "What makes you think she's trying to find Martha? She doesn't even know the woman."

Amanda swallowed. "She showed me an old snapshot...of her mother and a young man. A blond-haired man with green eyes. Summer's eyes."

Phillip. Summer had a picture of Sara and Phillip? Michael could feel the blood drain from his face.

"She said it was a picture of her parents."

His stomach churning, Michael asked, "Did she know her...?" Michael tried again, unable to bring himself to call Phillip her father. "Did she know the name of the man in the photograph?"

"I don't think so."

A small measure of relief washed over him. "Then what makes you think she's looking for Martha?"

"Because she told me she was looking for her grand-mother," Amanda said softly. "She said Sara told her the man in the photograph was her father and that his mother, her grandmother, was a very important lady who lived in New Orleans. She asked me to help her find her."

"What did you tell her?"

"I told her she would have to ask you."

She already had, months ago, and he'd thought he had convinced her that Sara had been mistaken. And he'd fool-ishly thought Summer had abandoned the idea.

"No matter how I feel about the situation, I would never have told her about Martha," Amanda informed him, her voice tinged with hurt. "Not without your permission."

Michael pulled Amanda to him and held her close. He squeezed his eyes shut. "I know." He kissed the top of her head.

After a moment Amanda pulled back slightly. "But I still think you should tell her. You know how important family is to Summer. She has a right to know."

What she said was true. He realized that, but he couldn't take that chance.

"Maybe if you talked to Martha, agreed to allow her to visit Summer—"

"No."

"But suppose she takes you to court—"

"I'll deal with it."

"Maybe if I—"

"I said, I'll handle it, Amanda. Alone. The last thing I need is for you to accuse me of using you again. I'm not going to give you another excuse to run away."

Amanda remained quiet for a moment. Then, slowly, she slipped her arms around his neck. "Does it look like I'm running away?" She gave him a smile so filled with love that he felt as though he'd been punched in the gut.

"Maybe you should be," he said before lowering his head and tasting her lips. But it was already too late, he realized, deepening the kiss. Now that he'd had a taste of her, knew what it was like to hold her in his arms, to hear her laughter, he wouldn't, couldn't, let her go.

At the sound of the doorbell, Michael released her. As he went to answer it, Amanda leaned her head back against the couch. She touched her swollen lips with unsteady fingertips, disappointed and at the same time grateful for the interruption. She'd never considered herself a particularly sensual being, yet with Michael she seemed to lose control.

"Amanda, this is Elsie Winters, my next-door neighbor," Michael said, entering the room. "Elsie, this is Amanda Bennett."

"Hello, Amanda. I've heard so much about you."

Amanda stood to greet the elderly brunette with laughing dark eyes. "How do you do?" she said, accepting the outstretched hand.

"Why, you're just as pretty as Summer said you were. She talks about you all the time," she went on. "I'm glad I finally got to meet you."

"The pleasure's mine, Ms. Winters."

"Elsie, dear. Call me Elsie. I feel as though I know you already."

"I called Elsie earlier and asked her if she'd keep an eye on Summer while I brought you home," Michael explained.

"You didn't have to do that," Amanda said. "I could have taken a taxi."

"Nonsense," Elsie told her. "You two run along. I'm just going to watch a little TV." Sitting down in the easy chair, she picked up the television remote control. Elsie clicked on the power button and a toothpaste commercial filled the screen.

"Nice meeting you, Ms.—Elsie."

"You, too, dear."

Michael put his arm around Amanda's shoulders and urged her toward the door. "I won't be long, Elsie."

"Take your time," Elsie mumbled as she kicked back in the chair and flipped the station to the Saturday night movie.

When they turned onto her street a short time later, Amanda said, "I like your neighbor. She seems nice."

"She is." He pulled up in front of her house and shut off the engine, then turned to her. "But her timing's lousy."

Amanda could feel the color rising to her cheeks, realizing just how involved she and Michael had been when Elsie had rung the bell. What would have happened if they hadn't been interrupted?

"I had a wonderful time today."

"So did I," she murmured.

"I never did get around to thanking you for rescuing me with those cupcakes."

"Yes, you did—several times. But I'm the one who should thank you. I had a terrific time. I'm glad I went."

"So am I." He took a strand of her hair and wrapped it around his index finger. Pausing, he looked her directly in the eyes. "Why did you come today? What made you change your mind?"

Amanda's heart pounded in her chest. "Summer," she said. And because I love you, she added silently.

"You're pretty fond of her, aren't you?"

"Yes," she answered softly. "I am."

"And what about her uncle? Are you fond of him, too?"

Amanda's throat grew thick and she struggled to swallow past the sudden lump. "Michael, I—"

"Because I'm nuts about you, Amanda." He pulled her close. "These past few days, not seeing you, talking to you...I was going crazy. You're all I could think about...the way you looked, the way you smelled, the way you felt in my arms. When I turned around in the kitchen today and saw you..." He took a deep breath. "And tonight when I kissed you..." He slid his fingers into her hair. Cupping her head, he brought her mouth a fraction from his.

Amanda moaned deep in her throat. She lifted her face for his kiss, needing the closeness as much as he.

His mouth devoured hers. And this time when he kissed her there was no gentleness, no teasing—only hunger, hot and demanding and raw.

He lifted his head slightly, his breath coming in quick, deep gasps. "Let's go inside," he said before slipping out of the car.

She heard the urgency in his voice, saw the need that mirrored her own. The realization thrilled her and frightened her at same time. Amanda shook her head, trying to clear the fuzziness as Michael helped her from the car.

When they reached her door, Amanda hesitated, suddenly afraid. She was in love with him and she was afraid—afraid of loving again, of opening herself up, of being hurt.

"Amanda?"

But would love be enough? Would it be worth the risk? "Michael, I—" She swallowed and tried to explain. "Don't you have to get back to Summer?"

Michael frowned. "Summer's fine. What's the matter?" he asked, his voice laced with concern.

She took a deep breath and tried again. "I can't think straight. And everything's been happening so fast."

"Not from where I'm standing. This thing between us has been there from the beginning."

"I know," she admitted. "It's just that I'm not sure I'm ready for us to... to become..."

"The word you're looking for is 'lovers.'"

She looked up at him, fearing she would find anger at her retreating tactics.

She found understanding instead. "It's nothing to be ashamed of," he told her. "Maybe for you everything does seem sudden. But not for me. I've known from the first time I set eyes on you that I wanted you, how good things could be between us. I've made love to you a thousand times in my dreams." He stroked her cheek tenderly. His eyes were filled with such longing it took her breath away. "I guess I'll just have to dream a little longer."

"Thank you for understanding," she whispered. She loved him; she wanted him, yet... Once they became lovers there would be no turning back.

"Just remember, love, I'm not a patient man. Don't ask me to wait too long."

Ten

—

Michael had lied to her. He *was* a patient man. Far more patient than she'd ever dreamed he would be. Far more patient than she was.

After weeks of tantalizing, breath-stealing kisses that ended at her front door, she'd been reduced to a mass of frustrated longings. Enough was enough. She was tired of waiting.

Amanda checked on the chicken and spaghetti. Satisfied, she returned to the dining room and dimmed the lights, then stood back to survey the table set intimately for two. She was through denying her feelings. She loved Michael. And she wanted him. It was as simple and as complicated as that. Now that she'd put everything into perspective, she realized Michael couldn't use her—not unless she allowed him to.

And she *wouldn't*. Sighing, Amanda thought of all those silent lectures she'd given herself, all the time she'd wasted steeling herself for proclamations of love and pleas to testify on his behalf at a custody hearing.

All her fears had been for nothing. And from his silence, she could only assume Michael had been right. Martha had decided not to follow through on her threat to sue for custody of Summer.

But Summer and Martha weren't her problem right now—Michael was. Adjusting one of the silver candle holders, Amanda smoothed the lacy tablecloth, then walked over to the stereo and turned it on.

After spending every free moment together for the past three weeks, she was more than ready to progress to the next stage in their relationship—becoming lovers. She'd made that much obvious.

So why had he backed off?

The soft sounds of a Righteous Brothers' melody filled the room as Amanda recalled the heated look in his eyes when he'd kissed her the previous night, the feel of his hard, muscled body pressed next to her own.

Amanda shuddered. He still wanted her. Of that much she was sure. And as far as she was concerned, they'd waited long enough. Tonight, if everything worked according to plan, she and Michael would become lovers.

The doorbell rang and Amanda's heart fluttered. Taking a deep breath, she smoothed the floral skirt of her strapless cotton dress and forced herself to take slow, measured steps.

"Hi," she said, opening the door.

"Hello." Standing in the doorway with his jacket hooked over one shoulder, Michael's eyes gleamed appreciatively as they swept over the soft pastel fabric that hugged her breasts and flared out at the waist. "All set?"

"Not quite," Amanda replied. "Why don't you come in for a minute and have a drink?" She stepped back, gesturing for him to enter.

Michael glanced at his watch. "We'll have to make it a quick one." He tossed his jacket onto a chair. "Our dinner reservation's for eight."

"Not anymore."

Michael turned around and arched his brow in question.

"I canceled the reservation," she explained, amazed at how calm she sounded. "I thought we'd have dinner here instead." Heart pounding, she walked into the living room.

Suddenly nervous, she stopped in front of the plate-glass window and watched the sun complete its descent. She could hear Michael come up behind her, smell the scent of his after-shave. A shiver of excitement ran through her and she touched the glass, feeling the sun's heat beneath her fingertips.

"Amanda?"

Turning, she smiled at him before moving beside the silver stand and ice bucket. She lifted the bottle of chilled champagne. "I'm afraid I've never quite gotten the hang of opening these things. Would you mind?"

Taking the bottle from her, Michael studied the expensive label a moment before looking up. "Are we celebrating something?"

Amanda smiled. They were celebrating the next stage of their affair. "You might say that."

He inserted the corkscrew into the bottle and began twisting it. "Are you going to let me in on what it is we're celebrating?"

"Oh, you'll find out soon enough."

Michael gave the opener a final twist then pulled. The cork shot out with a pop. And champagne, white and frothy, bubbled over the bottle's rim.

Amanda held out two tulip-shaped glasses. "I've been cooking all afternoon. I hope you're hungry."

"Starved."

"Good. We're having spaghetti."

"Spaghetti's one of my favorites." He filled the two strawberry-garnished glasses.

"I hope you don't mind the change in plans, but I really didn't want to be around other people tonight."

Michael paused a moment; his eyes burrowed into hers. "Since when have you become antisocial?" He took one of the glasses.

"Since I decided I wanted to be alone with you." She lifted her glass. "Shall we make a toast?"

"By all means. But since I'm not exactly sure what it is we're celebrating, why don't you do the honors?"

"All right. How about...to lovers."

Michael's eyes heated, darkening to the color of sapphires. He studied her mouth for what seemed like an eternity, then slid his gaze down her neck, her bare shoulders, to the tops of her breasts. Finally he brought his gaze back to hers. "To lovers," he said, tapping his glass to hers.

Heat curled inside her, spreading through her stomach, down between her thighs. Her heart thudded wildly. Watching Michael over the rim of her glass, Amanda sipped the champagne slowly. Feeling daring, she removed the strawberry from her glass and dipped it into the champagne. "Did you know strawberries enhance the flavor of champagne?" she asked.

"Is that so?"

She licked the tip of the ripe berry, then dipped it again. "Mmm-hmm. Something to do with the mingling of juices."

Michael stood frozen. Not a muscle moved—except for his eyes. His eyes devoured her mouth.

Amanda bit into the strawberry and savored the unique blend of fruit and wine. She licked her lips, catching the drops of juice and champagne with her tongue. When she met his eyes again, her heart leapt to her throat. She'd heard the term "naked desire" before but never had she seen it— and never had she expected it to be directed at her.

Encouraged by his response, Amanda set down her glass and took a step toward him. She lifted the piece of strawberry to his lips. "Would you like a taste?"

Michael caught her wrist and guided her hand to his mouth. She shivered as his tongue flicked across her fingertips. Still holding her wrist, he chewed the bit of fruit slowly, never once taking his eyes from her. "You're right, it does taste better this way." One by one, he licked the tips of her fingers, grazing the sensitized flesh with his teeth.

Her body trembling, Amanda leaned into him. "Michael," she whispered, wanting him, needing him. She caressed his cheek, his jaw. Reaching for his tie, she pulled it free.

Blood ran through his veins hot and thick as lava. Setting down his glass, Michael caught both of her wrists. "Do you know what you're doing?" he demanded through gritted teeth.

"Yes." Impatient to feel him, to touch him, she pulled her hands free and began loosening the buttons of his shirt.

"Amanda..." He imprisoned her hands once more, feeling the thread of control he'd been exercising for weeks begin to fray.

Amanda looked up into his eyes. "Please, Michael, don't make me wait any longer. Make love to me."

Michael stiffened. Silently he cursed his own weakness. He'd realized weeks ago that he wanted more than a casual affair with Amanda and that possessing her body would never be enough. That's why he'd taken his time, tried not to rush her. He wanted her love. He wanted her trust.

At the dark look in his eyes, the stiff line of his jaw, Amanda's resolve weakened. Had she made a mistake? Did Michael not want her?

Michael noted the flash of doubt creep into her eyes and his thin thread of control snapped. He pulled her into his arms. "Be sure this is what you want, Amanda. Because once you're mine, I'll never let you go."

"It's what I want," she murmured, relief rushing through her. She slid her hands up his chest, around his neck, and lifted her mouth for his kiss. "You're what I want."

Groaning, Michael took possession of her mouth. He thrust his tongue between her lips and savored the sweetness that had tempted and tormented him for months.

Amanda met his hunger, giving reign to her own desires. When he released her mouth, she whimpered. She pressed her body against him, wanting, needing to be closer still.

Michael shuddered at the soft, feminine sounds she was making. His own breathing grew ragged as he fought for some semblance of control.

A thrill of pleasure spread through her at Michael's response. She kissed his jaw, his throat, while her fingers worked at the remaining buttons of his shirt. Pulling the fabric free of his pants, Amanda spread the shirt open and ran her fingers in the thicket of chest hair. She brought her mouth to the warm, tanned skin and tasted the flesh she'd exposed.

Michael groaned. "Do you have any idea what you're doing to me?"

Amanda looked up at him out of dark, smoky eyes. She traced his mouth with her tongue. "The same thing you're doing to me, I hope."

Her boldness was the final straw. Desire, held carefully in check, exploded inside him. Slowly and with a thoroughness that brought both pleasure and pain, Michael kissed her lips, her chin, her neck, the sweet silken skin of her shoulders. He drew his finger over the tip of one breast, feeling the bud harden under his touch. When she arched her body toward him, he pulled her back into his arms.

Amanda ran her fingers down his back, along his buttocks, and Michael made a guttural sound that caused her pulse to scatter even more. He kissed her again, devouring her mouth, her very senses. When he cupped her and cradled her against his desire, Amanda cried out, "Michael, please."

Michael tore his mouth from hers. "Where's your bedroom?" he asked, his voice tight with need.

"No," she managed to say through love-drugged senses. "Make love to me here. Now."

Michael eased down her zipper and her dress pooled at her feet. She stepped out of the circle of flowers and kicked it aside. Moonlight spilled through the window, bathing her in its glow. For a moment Michael could only stare. Standing before him in only a wisp of lavender lace and sheer hose, she looked like a goddess. Her breasts, the color of rich cream, were full, firm, and begging to be kissed. Unable to resist, he bent his head and tasted one dark rosy tip.

Amanda gasped as waves of pleasure shot through her. Reaching for his belt, she unfastened it quickly and fumbled with his zipper.

Capturing her hands, Michael brought them to his mouth. Slowly, gently, he kissed her knuckles. "I want you," he said, his voice thick with desire. "So much that a day hasn't gone by that I haven't closed my eyes and wished I could bury myself inside you. And it's taking every ounce of control I have left not to take you this very minute. Standing up."

Amanda's knees grew weak at the urgency in his voice. Pulling her hands free, she reached for him and closed her fingers around his hard length. "Then take me. Here. Now."

Michael squeezed his eyes shut a moment and drew a steadying breath. "Heaven help me. I want to. But I've waited a long time for tonight and I'm not going to rush it." He swallowed as the need inside him grew. "I'm going to savor every moment of making you mine." And when he was finished, she would belong to him forever.

He kissed her lips. Slowly, thoroughly. "So beautiful. So perfect," he murmured. He kissed and licked and nibbled at her ears, her neck, her shoulders, setting off trails of sensation wherever he touched. Arms locked around one another, they sank to the carpet.

Amanda tugged at the waistband of his slacks, but Michael caught her hands and pinned them over her head. "Patience, love," he whispered as he continued the torment to her senses.

Sweat broke out across his brow, but Michael strained to hold his desire in check. He loved her, wanted her, but her pleasure was more important than his.

Just when she thought she would go mad from wanting, Michael's mouth closed over the tip of her breast. Amanda moaned, writhing under the exquisite sensations.

Releasing her hands, he filled his palms with her breasts and kissed his way down her rib cage to the soft indentation of her navel.

Amanda whimpered.

He soothed her with another kiss as he unhooked the stocking from her garter belt. He removed the silk from first one leg, then the next, slowly kissing the skin as he exposed it. Once he had kissed the soles of both feet and discarded the scraps of lace, he worked his way upward again.

Michael paused at the nest of blond silk that shielded her and fought the urge to make her his now. He wanted to make it perfect for her, for them. Forcing himself to go slowly, he kicked off his shoes, then shed his slacks and briefs. He reached for the glass of champagne. Staring into her eyes, glazed with passion, Michael poured a few drops of the wine in her navel, then lowered his head.

Amanda gasped. Her head moved from side to side as Michael's tongue licked and caressed her. "Please, Michael," she pleaded, half mad with longing.

"Not yet, love. Not yet."

Michael dipped his fingers into the champagne then stroked the lips of her femininity.

Amanda cried out and arched her hips toward him. He stroked her again, slowly torturing and pleasuring her.

As she watched, Michael brought his fingers to his mouth, then licked their tips. "*You* enhance the flavor of champagne," he told her before lowering his head once more and tasting her honeyed sweetness.

"Michael." Amanda shuddered as wave after wave washed over her, sending her hurtling into a wind-tossed sea of sensation. Helpless against the onslaught, she clung to Michael, pulling him with her into the tempest.

Already weak with desire, Amanda's soft, hungry noises drove Michael over the edge. Lifting his head, he moved between her legs and drove into her warmth.

Amanda gasped as he filled her emptiness.

"I'm sorry, love. I meant to go slow," he managed to say through labored breaths. But he'd wanted her too badly, loved her too much, and he'd been unable to slow his body's urgent rhythm.

"Don't stop," she cried when he started to withdraw. She wrapped her arms around him, urging him faster, deeper.

Michael thrust into her, driving them to the edge of the storm. Caught in the rush of sensations, she lifted her hips to meet his as the waves engulfed her.

"Amanda." He called out her name and plunged into her a final time. Arching her body to meet his, Amanda followed him heart-first into the eye of the storm.

By the time the two of them sat down to dinner, the chicken was cold and the spaghetti tasted like rubber.

Not that Michael seemed to notice.

She studied him from across the table. He ate the meal with the same intensity and thoroughness that he made love, she thought. A tiny shiver went through her as Amanda watched the hands and mouth that had given her such pleasure.

"That was delicious," he said, pushing back from the table.

Amanda blinked and pulled her thoughts back to the present. "It would have been if we'd eaten it earlier."

He shot her a wicked grin. "I'm not complaining."

"Neither am I," Amanda said, returning his smile. Their lovemaking *had* been wonderful. She'd never considered herself a sensuous creature, but Michael made her feel like one. Even now, just looking at him—sitting there in only his slacks, his dark hair all mussed from her fingers, his eyes smoky and hooded, she could feel desire stir in the pit of her stomach once again.

Michael stood and her gaze drifted to the dark V of hair that disappeared inside his unbuttoned slacks. Amanda's mouth went dry.

"Since you cooked, why don't I clean the kitchen?" Michael picked up his plate.

Amanda shook her head to clear it, then quickly came to her feet. "I'll take care of these. You sit down and relax. I'll only be a minute." She took the plate from him and carried it into the kitchen. She turned on the water. "How about some dessert?" she called out as she rinsed the plates and loaded them into the dishwasher.

"Sounds good."

"It'll just take me a second to put on some coffee and I have this great strawberry shor—" Amanda drew in her breath as Michael slid his arms around her waist and pulled her back against him. Her hands stilled under the running water. Squeezing her eyes shut, she delighted in the feel of his hardness pressed against her.

Michael nuzzled her neck while he untied the belt of her robe. As the sash fell to her feet, the folds of silk parted, leaving her naked to his touch. He kissed the sensitive spot behind her ear.

Amanda shuddered.

"I had something else in mind for dessert," he murmured huskily as his hand cupped her breast before moving slowly down her stomach and then between her thighs.

His fingers teased her, tormented her, until Amanda thought she would scream. When he slipped one finger inside her and stroked her sensitized flesh, Amanda held her breath.

The silverware fell from her fingers, clattering loudly in the sink as the first ripple of pleasure hit her. Knees weak, Amanda gripped the edge of the basin as wave after wave of sensation rolled over her, the warmth flowing like honey from her secret place.

Reaching across her, Michael shut off the faucet, then turned Amanda around to face him. He slid one arm beneath her knees and picked her up. "Why don't we finish the rest of our meal in bed?"

Still in a sensual fog, she curled her arms around his neck and rested her head against his shoulder as he carried her up the stairs.

Once inside her bedroom, Michael used one hand to pull back the comforter covering the brass bed while he continued to hold her. Gently he placed her on the bed, then stepped back.

Unable to find her voice, Amanda held out her arms to him.

Michael's eyes smoldered, burned her with the hunger she read in them. Still he made no motion to accept what she was so clearly offering.

"Tell me what you want, Amanda," he said, his voice thick, husky with desire.

"You," she whispered. "I want you."

Groaning, he stripped away his slacks and briefs in one
swift movement and joined her on the bed. He sculpted her
body with his hands, drawing her arms above her head,
capturing both of her hands in one of his. "Say it again. Tell
me you want me," he repeated.

Beads of perspiration broke out across his brow and
Amanda realized what his restraint was costing him, what
it was costing her.

"I want you, Michael," she whispered. "I want to feel
you inside me. All of you—now."

She didn't have to ask him again.

He moved between her thighs, buried himself inside her,
filling her with his hardness, his warmth, his burning need.

Amanda arched her body beneath his, striving to match
his rhythm as she moved closer and closer toward the source
of his heat. Just when she thought she could take no more,
a new tide of pleasure flooded her, hurling her headfirst into
a whirlwind of sensation. Clutching his shoulders, she cried
out his name.

Seconds later Michael followed her into the vortex, calling out her name before his own body collapsed atop her.

By the time her heart rate had returned to normal,
Amanda could feel the smile stealing over his lips as he cradled her body against him and drifted off to sleep.

He was still smiling when Amanda opened her eyes several hours later and found Michael lying in bed beside her,
propped up on one elbow, watching her. "Morning," he
said, brushing his lips against hers.

"Morning." She stretched and suddenly became aware of
sore muscles. "What time is it?"

"Early. The sun's not even up yet." He swept a strand of
hair away from her eyes.

Amanda yawned. She glanced over at the clock on the
bedside table. The hands pointed to a few minutes past five.
"What are you doing up so early?"

"Watching you sleep," he said softly.

"That can't be any fun."

"Quite the contrary. I like watching you." He caressed
her cheek. "And I especially like waking up to you."

At the serious note in his voice, Amanda looked into his eyes. But instead of the desire she expected to find, she saw what looked like determination.

Determination? The thought made her nervous and she pulled the sheet up to cover her breasts.

"In fact, I was thinking that I wouldn't mind waking up to you every morning. In fact, I think I'd like it—very much."

Telling herself she was being foolish, Amanda tried to shake her uneasiness. "Sure. That's what you say now, but before you know it, you'll be complaining I hog the covers."

"If we were together, you wouldn't need any covers. I'd keep you warm." To prove his point, he pulled away the sheet and covered her breast with his hand.

The heat from his fingers seemed to burn right through her and she could feel her body quiver. When she looked at his eyes, Amanda's heart fluttered. Trying once more to break the tension, she joked, "That's a tempting offer, Mr. Grayson, but just wait until the first hard freeze hits and—"

"Marry me, Amanda."

Stunned, Amanda blinked, unable to believe she'd heard him correctly.

"I'm in love with you. I have been for months."

Was it true? Could he really be in love with her? For herself? She sat up, pulling the sheet over her breasts once again. "Michael, I don't know what to say."

He smiled at her, his expression hopeful. "How about 'I love you, too' and 'yes, I'll marry you, Michael.'"

Amanda didn't know what to say. She couldn't say anything.

At her silence, his smile faded. "Was I wrong in thinking that last night meant something special to you, too?"

"No." She rushed to assure him, unable to bear the hurt look in his eyes. "You weren't wrong. It's just...I hadn't thought about getting married."

"Why not? That's what two people usually do when they love each other. Isn't it?"

How could she explain? Make him understand? She loved him, wanted to be with him, but she didn't want marriage. Marriage held too many risks, risks she still wasn't sure she wanted to take—at least, not yet.

"Well, isn't it?" Michael demanded.

"Not always. Marriage isn't for everyone, Michael." Least of all her. "Some people are better off just having an affair."

Michael frowned. "Is that what you want, Amanda? An affair?"

He made the word sound dirty, cheap. Deliberately, Amanda tipped her chin up. "Yes."

"I see." He paused a moment. "Well, I'm afraid an affair's not good enough—at least, not for me. If that's all I'd wanted, I would have taken you to bed weeks ago."

She started to protest, but Michael silenced her with a look. "Don't bother denying it. We both know I could have had you anytime I wanted during the past month."

She didn't deny it because it was true. "Then why didn't you?"

"Because I didn't want just your body and a few meaningless romps between the sheets. I wanted you."

Amanda's heart pounded. She wanted to believe him. But hadn't Adam told her the same things? Hadn't he sworn that he'd loved and wanted her, too, when all he'd wanted was a mother for his daughter?

"I love you."

She squeezed her eyes shut against the painful memories. Were Michael's motives any different? After all, there had been the problem with Summer. And what about Martha Winthrop? And her threat of a custody suit?

Does it really matter? a voice deep inside her asked.

"Do you love me?" he asked.

"Yes," she admitted. She did love him and this time what she felt was a thousand times deeper and more dangerous than what she'd ever felt for Adam. She stared at him, realizing that the risk this time was greater; but then, so were the rewards.

Taking her by the shoulders, Michael gave her a slight shake. "Say it, Amanda."

"I love you."

"Again."

"I love you."

He dragged her into his arms and kissed her roughly, deeply, desperately. "And you're going to marry me," he ordered when he finally released her mouth.

"Yes," she whispered, knowing she would and praying she wasn't making a mistake.

"You're mine now," he told her as he stripped away the sheet and cupped her breasts possessively. He pinned her with his eyes. "And as soon as Summer gets back from camp, we're going to make it legal."

She wanted to protest, to tell him there was no need to rush things. But when his teeth closed over her nipple, she arched forward automatically, winding her fingers through his hair, holding his head to her breast.

Moments later when he moved between her legs, all thoughts of denial faded as she became lost once more in the sensual storm of Michael's lovemaking.

Eleven

"**I** still don't see what the big rush is," Amanda complained. "Why can't we just be engaged for a while?"

"Because it doesn't make any sense to wait." After locking the car, Michael took Amanda's hand. Together they started across the school parking lot to join the other parents waiting to pick up their children from summer camp. "Besides," he said, slanting her a seductive glance that sent shivers up her spine, "I want you in my bed *every* night."

"You've been in *my* bed every night," she reminded him.

And her shower, and her couch, and her pool. Even on her kitchen counter. Amanda smiled. Their lovemaking had been hot, spontaneous and wildly passionate since that first night a week ago.

Michael grinned. "I know. And I've enjoyed every minute of it, too." Stopping a few feet from where the other parents were gathered, Michael kissed the tip of her nose. "But Summer coming home changes things."

"I know," Amanda said, sighing. It meant that Michael would no longer be staying overnight. And she was going to miss him. In addition to the wonderful lovemaking, she'd quickly grown accustomed to waking up with him beside her.

"I warned you I wasn't big on patience. And where you're concerned I have even less. I have no intention of spending one more night away from you than I have to."

Amanda's heart tripped a little faster, as it always did when Michael looked at her with such hunger in his eyes. She felt as though she were in a wonderful dream and she didn't ever want to wake up. Never in her life had she been the object of such love, such desire. Knowing that she was made her feel light-headed.

"So it's settled. We get married next week like we planned. Okay?"

"Okay," she agreed as they joined the others at the edge of the school walkway.

She had to stop being foolish and quit waiting for the ax to fall, Amanda told herself. She loved Michael and he loved her. And they were going to be married. At least this time she was being married for herself.

"Amanda. Michael." Sister Mary Grace waved. Excusing herself from another couple, she made her way over to them.

"Hello, Sister." Michael shook her hand. "It's good to see you again."

"It's nice to see you, too. Here to pick up Summer?"

"Yes, we are."

Amanda gave her friend a hug. "I called you at the convent last week, but they told me you were on retreat."

"I was. I just got back this morning."

"How are you?" Amanda asked the tiny nun.

"I'm fine. And I don't need to ask how you are. You look wonderful."

"Thanks. I feel pretty wonderful," Amanda admitted, acknowledging that a large measure of her newfound happiness was due to Michael.

"Well, it certainly shows." Sister Mary Grace smiled, then shifted her attention to Michael. "You're looking pretty chipper yourself, Mr. Grayson."

"That's because I'm feeling pretty chipper, Sister." Michael slipped his arm around Amanda's shoulders and gave her a look filled with warmth and love. "Amanda and I are getting married."

Sister Mary Grace beamed. She clasped her hands together. "Why, that's wonderful news. Congratulations." She hugged them both.

"Amanda and I would like it very much if you would come to the wedding, Sister. It's not going to be very big. Just Summer, a few close friends and you, if you can make it."

"I'd be honored, Michael. Thank you for asking me. When's the big day?"

"Next Saturday at two," he informed her.

Sister Mary Grace lifted her brow, her surprise evident. "You certainly don't waste any time, do you?"

"Can't afford to. Not with this lady." Michael hugged Amanda a little closer. "Getting her to fall in love with me took quite a bit of work and I don't mind telling you, it was one tough battle. But, fortunately, my strategy paid off."

He smiled, obviously pleased with himself. "Anyway, once she agreed to marry me, I decided the smartest thing I could do was get a ring on her finger before she had a chance to change her mind."

"I knew you were a smart man," Sister Mary Grace said, laughing.

Amanda sniffed, not exactly thrilled to have her friend and the man she loved discussing the winning of her heart as though it were a battle. "He's not all that smart or he wouldn't be bragging about his strategy. After all, we're not married yet."

Michael's smile faltered. "Amanda, love, I didn't mean anything... That is, I was only joking with the Sister."

Amanda immediately regretted her flip comeback. She couldn't bear to see the look of doubt on his face. "I know."

Out of the corner of her eye, Amanda spied the big yellow school bus turning into the lot. "Come on, Mr. Strategy. There's Summer's bus now."

"We'll be in touch about the wedding," Michael told her. He reached for Amanda's hand. "Right now, there's a little girl we're going to make very happy when we tell her she's got a wedding to help us plan."

Happy didn't even begin to describe Summer's reaction. She was ecstatic. "Do I get to call you Aunt Amanda now?" she asked over dinner that evening.

"If you'd like. Or you can just call me Amanda. It's up to you."

Summer paused for a moment and tilted her head. "I heard Sister Mary Grace call you Mandy once. I like that name. Can I call you Aunt Mandy?"

Amanda laughed, her heart swelling at the child's obvious happiness about their news. "Of course."

"Are we going to have a big wedding?" Summer asked before biting into her hamburger.

"Nope. Just you, Mr. Dave, Sister Mary Grace and a few other friends," Michael replied.

"What about Aunt Mandy's family?"

"Amanda's parents are out of the country right now."

"They can't be here for the wedding," Amanda explained, a little sad that her parents wouldn't be able to share her happiness. "But they're going to come visit us at the end of the summer when they get back to the States."

Michael reached for Amanda's hand and squeezed it. "Do you mind that they can't be here? I know I insisted on getting married next week, but if it's important to you that your parents be here—"

"It's not," she said, touched by his sensitivity. "Knowing you love me is what's important."

"I do," he assured her, kissing her knuckles. The love shone in his eyes.

"When you and Uncle Mike get married, does that mean your mom and dad will be my family, too?" Summer asked.

"Yes," Amanda said, smiling as she turned her attention back to Summer. "They'll be your great-aunt and uncle."

"Oh." Summer picked up a french fry and dipped it in catsup. "I wish they could be my grandparents. Michelle has

grandparents. She gets to stay over at their house sometimes, and they bring her back presents when they go on
trips."

Amanda's heart twisted at the longing in Summer's voice.
"You know, Summer, my parents have always wanted
grandchildren. I bet they would love for you to call them
Grandma and Grandpa."

"That's a great idea," Michael added.

Amanda glanced over at Michael, disturbed by how anxious he sounded.

"But they wouldn't really be my grandparents, would
they?"

"No," Amanda admitted. "But I bet they'd be very
happy if you thought of them as though they were. I just
know they're going to love you."

"If I could find my real grandmother, I bet she would
love me, too."

Michael set down his fork. His face pulled into a frown.
"Summer, let's not start that again."

"But, Uncle Mike, if I could find my grandmother—"

Michael pushed back his chair and stood. "That's
enough! I don't want to hear any more of this nonsense."

Summer folded her arms across her chest. Her head
dropped.

Sighing, Michael came around the table and knelt beside
his niece. "Honey, your mom made me your guardian because I was her only relative and she entrusted you to me.
Maybe someday Amanda and I'll be lucky and have children. Then you'll have some cousins. But right now, you're
going to have to settle for us. We're the only family you've
got."

Amanda's heart ached for them both. If only Michael
would relent about Martha. She swallowed and went to
crouch next to the child. "We love you, Summer."

Summer looked up at Amanda, her eyes brimming with
tears. "And I love you. Both of you."

"We want you to be happy, honey," Michael told her.
"Do you think you can be happy with us?"

Summer flung one arm around her uncle's neck and the other around Amanda's. "Yes," she whispered. "I'll be happy. I promise."

Even though the rest of the evening was pleasant enough, the day had lost its sparkle. Amanda tucked Summer into bed and kissed her good-night.

It just wasn't fair, Amanda thought. No matter what had happened in the past, Summer deserved to at least know she had a grandmother. Somehow she had to convince Michael of that.

"Michael," she said while cuddled with him a short time later in front of the television.

"Hmm?" He clicked the button on the remote control device, switching the channel to the ten o'clock news.

"I think you're making a mistake by not telling Summer about Martha."

"There's nothing to tell," he said dismissively.

"You know that's not true. What if Summer finds out that her grandmother wanted to see her and you forbade it?"

Michael stiffened. "She won't find out. No one even knows about her connection to Martha except you and Dave. Dave won't say anything. And you gave me your word you wouldn't tell her either."

"And I won't. But I think you should."

Michael removed his arm from around her. "Look, Amanda, I don't want to argue with you about this."

Amanda sighed. "Michael, if I didn't think it was so important, I'd drop it. But you know how much it means to Summer to have a family. You're not being fair to her."

"I'm doing what's best for her. She'd be better off without any relatives than to claim Martha Winthrop as her grandmother."

"Your hate and bitterness for the Winthrops is making you blind. And foolish. Suppose Martha decides to sue for custody, after all? What if by some chance she should win?" Amanda couldn't finish, too afraid to put into words the possibility that Martha might keep Summer from them just as Michael was now keeping the child from her.

The muscle in Michael's jaw ticked wildly. Something flashed in his eyes and then that steely look of determination was back. "Trust me. Martha doesn't stand a chance of getting custody of Summer."

His expression was as hard as granite. It was the same look she'd seen the night he'd insisted she marry him. "This war between me and the Winthrops has been going on for a long time, but it's going to be over soon. And when it is, I promise you, I'm going to be the winner."

It was there again—that cold confidence. It made her uneasy. "How can you be so sure?"

"I told you, I'm a good strategist. And I have the element of surprise on my side." Looking into her eyes, Michael eased Amanda down onto the couch and stretched his body over hers. "Now, enough talk about Martha Winthrop. I haven't had a real kiss in hours."

Amanda slipped her arms around his neck and as her body responded to his touch, her uneasiness started to fade.

He slipped his hands beneath her blouse and cupped her breasts. "Heaven help me. I don't know how I'm going to get through the night, let alone the next week without you," he whispered before lowering his head.

Amanda arched her body toward him as his mouth and hands worked their magic. Soon, Martha Winthrop and custody battles were the last thing on her mind as Amanda lost herself in the pleasure of his love.

"Hi," Amanda greeted Summer as she let herself into the house with the key Michael had given her.

"Hi, Aunt Mandy."

Amanda dropped the boxes of books and photographs she'd brought from her house onto the floor and flopped down onto the couch. "It's an oven out there," Amanda complained, wiping beads of perspiration from her brow. As much as she loved New Orleans, the heat and humidity were stifling.

"What's all that stuff?" Summer asked, already peeking inside the cartons.

"Just a few things I didn't want to send to storage." Because of her house's small size, she and Michael had decided the only sensible thing to do would be for her to move into his house until they could find a place to buy together. "Where's your uncle?"

"In the study on the phone," Summer said, flipping through a photo album she'd unearthed from one of the boxes.

"Would you be a sweetheart and put these boxes upstairs for me while I tell him I'm here?"

"Sure." Picking up one of the lightweight cartons, Summer headed for the stairs.

Amanda moved down the hall, stopping outside Michael's study. With the door ajar and Michael standing with his back to her, she took a moment to look at the man she loved. She still couldn't believe in two days' time they would be husband and wife.

"I know that," Michael snapped. He shoved a hand through his hair.

Amanda smiled at the familiar gesture, thinking how much she enjoyed running her fingers through that head of dark hair.

"Well, reschedule it, then." Michael paced the length of his desk. "Dammit, Dave. I'm getting married day after tomorrow and I don't want this hanging over my head."

Barely registering his words, Amanda concentrated on how tanned his skin was against the white of his shirt where he'd opened the collar and rolled up his sleeves. She smiled, knowing firsthand that Michael's tan extended over every inch of him.

"Tomorrow at ten? Hold on. Let me check my schedule." He turned then and saw her; and the harsh lines of his face softened. "Hi—" he covered the receiver with one hand "—I'll be through here in a second."

"Take your time," Amanda told him. She leaned against the door.

Michael patted his shirt pocket, then began searching the top of his desk. Frowning, he said, "Hang on a second, Dave. I can't find the darn thing."

"What are you looking for?" Amanda asked, coming closer.

"My appointment book." He glanced around the room. "I must have left it in my coat pocket."

"Where's your coat?"

"I think I threw it across the back of the couch when I came in. The book should be in the inside pocket."

"I'll get it," Amanda told him. "Say hello to Dave for me and tell him he'd better not be late Saturday."

Humming, Amanda returned to the living room. She spotted Michael's navy jacket immediately. Picking it up, she spread open the coat. A white envelope was sticking out of the pocket.

The marriage license, Amanda thought, and took out the document. She unfolded the paper.

"State of Louisiana. Parish of Orleans." Amanda scanned the petition.

"In the case of Martha Stallings Winthrop Versus Michael Patrick Grayson, you are hereby ordered to appear in court on the twenty-eighth of June, to determine the custody of Summer Grayson, child of..."

Amanda could feel the color drain from her face. She searched for the date of service. June fourteen. Two days before Michael had asked her to marry him.

She sank to the couch and stared at the Court summons, not wanting to believe what she saw. Blinking back tears, she read through the pleadings. The dry prose set out how eight years earlier a child had been born to Sara Grayson and Phillip Winthrop and had been given the name Summer Grayson. That Phillip Winthrop had died and Sara Grayson had taken the child and left the country. How Sara Grayson was now deceased and that Martha Winthrop wanted custody of her grandchild.

Snatches of conversations came back to her.

Trust me. Martha doesn't stand a chance of getting custody of Summer.

This war between me and the Winthrops is going to be over soon and I promise you, I'm going to win...

I told you, I'm a good strategist. Besides, I have a secret weapon . . .

He'd used her. Michael had used her in his battle to retain custody of Summer. *She* had been his element of surprise in the war with Martha Winthrop. Her hands trembled, her eyes blurred as she looked down at the petition before letting it fall to the floor.

She covered her face with her hands. The signs had been there all along, only she'd been too blinded by her love for him to see it.

"Amanda, did you find it?" Michael called from the doorway.

At the sound of his voice, Amanda snatched up his jacket and dug in the pocket for the appointment book. Brushing back tears, she carried the little black book into his study.

"What took you so long? Did you have trouble finding—" The smile in his eyes died. "Amanda, what's wrong?" he asked, his voice filled with concern.

"Here's your appointment book." She tossed the book onto the center of his desk. "And since you've got your lawyer on the phone, you'd better make sure he's got June twenty-eighth blocked out on his calendar for the custody hearing."

Michael paled beneath his tan. "Dave, I'll call you back." He hurriedly hung up the phone.

"How silly of me," Amanda said, feeling slightly hysterical. "Dave already knows, doesn't he? Everyone knows— except me."

"Amanda, I can explain."

"Can you, Michael?" Pain and bitterness drove her. "Can you explain why your marriage proposal came only two days after you found out Martha was suing you for custody of Summer?"

"That had nothing to do with my asking you to marry me."

"No? And I suppose the fact that you bullied me into setting the wedding only days before you're due in court had nothing to do with it, either?"

"It didn't!"

"And all that talk about battles and strategies and secret weapons . . ." Amanda's voice broke and she choked back a sob. "I'm your secret weapon, aren't I, Michael? Aren't I?"

"No."

"You planned to use me to beat Martha, didn't you? That's why you asked me to marry you."

"That's not true! I love you." He started toward her. "I know how it looks—"

"Don't touch me!" She held out her hands to keep him at bay. "When were you going to tell me about the lawsuit, Michael? After the ceremony? On our wedding night?"

"That's not the way it was."

His expression was thunderous, but still she pushed. "Or maybe you were going to tell me after you'd made love to me, when I was too sated by your lovemaking to care."

Michael grabbed her by the shoulders. "Stop it, Amanda. Stop it! You don't know what you're saying."

She could hear the anger in his voice, see the fury in his eyes as his fingers bit into her arms, but she couldn't stop. The pain was too great. "Tell me, Michael. Was that the plan? Was that when you were going to convince me to go with you to the courtroom and parade our perfect little family in front of the judge?"

Amanda laughed, but there was no joy in the sound.

Michael dragged her into his arms, crushing her against him. "No!" The word was a sob torn from his throat. "You're wrong. I love you. The custody suit has nothing to do with us."

Amanda struggled in his arms. No match against his strength, she finally went limp against him. Now that she'd vented her rage, the tears were threatening again. She needed to get away, to hide and lick her wounds in private. "Let go of me," she said in a voice as cold as a Boston December.

"Not until you let me explain."

"I'm not interested in your explanations. I just want to get out of here and forget you, forget that you were ever a part of my life."

"I won't let you go." He held her at arm's length and looked into her eyes. "I can't let you go. You *are* my life.

Without you, I have no life. You own my heart, Amanda. Please don't throw it away.''

He sounded so sincere, looked so crushed, Amanda could feel herself weakening.

"You were right. In the beginning, I guess I did set out to use you. I'd been toying with the idea that if I were married, my chances of keeping Summer would be better.''

He swallowed. "I was already attracted to you and you weren't exactly indifferent to me. When I saw how much you cared for Summer, how crazy she was about you, I figured, why not? Marrying you seemed like the perfect answer to everything. Everyone would come out ahead. Only it didn't work out that way.''

Amanda tried to steel herself to the crippling pain his words caused.

"All my plans to make you fall in love with me kept backfiring. I knew you were attracted to me, but you kept turning me down and I couldn't figure out why. I almost abandoned the idea a dozen times, but I couldn't get you out of my mind.''

He laughed, the sound hollow and mocking. "I told myself Summer was the reason I couldn't just walk away from you, but Summer was the last person I was thinking about when we were together. And every time I kissed you, it became harder and harder to let you go.

"That night after we ran into the Winthrops, I knew I'd fallen in love with you. I was going to confess everything to you the night we met at the coffeehouse and tell you how I felt. But then you told me about your ex-husband, how he had used you. I knew if I told you then, I'd lose you for good.''

His eyes were pleading as they met hers. "That night, when you told me to get out of your life, you were so distant, so untouchable afterward. I realized that I didn't dare tell you the truth—not until I got the custody issue behind me. Otherwise, I knew you'd never believe that I loved you. That it was really *you* I loved and not what help I thought you might bring to me in a custody hearing.

"Then you showed up here the afternoon of the school fair and I realized I couldn't wait that long. I told myself if I could get you to fall in love with me first, when I did tell you the truth, I stood a better chance of you forgiving me."

Was it possible? Could he truly love her as he claimed? For herself? A ribbon of hope began to unfurl inside her.

"I didn't mean to rush you. I'd planned for us to become lovers and gradually work up to marriage. But that first night you were so responsive and after you went to sleep in my arms, I knew I couldn't wait. And I asked you to marry me. But you started talking about having an affair and I got scared. I pushed you. When you said yes . . . I was afraid you'd change your mind. That's why I insisted we marry right away."

"But why didn't you tell me about the custody suit after I agreed to marry you?"

"For the same reason I didn't tell you in the first place. The suit had nothing to do with my wanting to marry you, but I was afraid you wouldn't believe me. That you would think that it did. Believe me, Amanda, I never ever intended to ask you to go with me to the hearing."

"But all that talk about strategy," Amanda said. "And you sounded so confident that you could win."

"I had reason to be. Phillip Winthrop isn't listed as Summer's father on her birth certificate and Sara had named me guardian in her will."

"But if that was enough, why were you so worried about the custody suit in the first place?"

"Because I wasn't sure if that was enough. I didn't think Martha Winthrop would want the scandal, but I couldn't be sure. She has a lot of clout in this city and I didn't trust her not to call in some favors from her friends on the bench."

"But you're not afraid of her now?"

"No." He paused a moment as though struggling with some inner battle. "A couple of weeks ago, I finally got around to going through Sara's things. I came across a packet of letters she had saved from Phillip. One of them was written after Sara got pregnant. Phillip told her he loved her and knew the right thing for him to do was to break away from his family and marry her. But he was afraid. In the letter, he seemed disgusted with himself because he was so weak. Phillip blamed his parents. His mother mostly— for making him so dependent upon her financially and emotionally. He said he felt like a cripple and that Sara deserved better. The rest of the letter was kind of disjointed, it seemed to ramble, but at the end Phillip said his only consolation was knowing that in deserting Sara he could ensure that his child would never grow up to be a coward like him. Because his child would never live under Martha's thumb.''

''Michael, it sounds almost like a . . . a . . .''

''A suicide note,'' he finished. ''I know. That's what I thought, too. A couple of days after Phillip was killed in a car wreck, Sara received a letter from him. I think it was *that* letter. She never would tell me what it said, but I remember she was pretty broken up at the time.''

''You were going to give that letter to the judge,'' she said, realizing now why Michael had been so confident he could win. He had planned to use the letter to convince the court that not even Phillip had wanted his mother to have Summer.

''I was at first,'' he admitted. ''But I changed my mind. I couldn't go through with it. As much as I dislike the woman, I couldn't let her spend the rest of her life wondering if she'd caused her son to kill himself. No one deserves that kind of hell, not even her.''

''Oh, Michael.'' Amanda threw her arms around his neck and held him close.

He hugged her tight for a moment, then set her away from him. ''That's why I called Dave. To have him arrange a meeting with Martha. I did a lot of thinking about what you said the other night, about my not being fair to Summer. I'd decided to tell Summer about Martha being her grandmother. I was going to try to work something out with Martha . . . where she could see Summer.'' His eyes searched her face. ''Please believe me, Amanda. I love you. And I need you. But not for Summer, for myself.''

When he pulled her into his arms, Amanda let the tears fall, but this time, they were tears of joy.

After Michael had kissed away the last of her tears and her doubts, he asked, "Will you help me break the news to Summer?"

"Yes," Amanda whispered. Holding his hand, they went upstairs in search of the little girl.

"Summer?" Amanda poked her head into the child's room. It was empty. "That's odd, she's not here. Michael, check your bedroom. I asked her to move some things in there for me."

But that room was empty, too. Amanda spied one of the cartons on the floor. "She carried this up for me. Maybe she went down to get the other one."

The other carton was sitting in the living room where Amanda had left it, but there was still no sign of Summer.

Trying not to panic, Amanda helped Michael search the rest of the house and the yard. When Summer still hadn't turned up at any of the neighbors' homes, both she and Michael were frantic.

Where can she be? Amanda kept asking herself. Pacing the room, she pushed aside the curtain and looked out into the yard once more while praying for a glimpse of Summer.

All she saw was the sun setting, another reminder that neither she nor Michael had seen the child for several hours. "Where could she have disappeared to?"

"I don't know," Michael said, coming to stand behind her. "But I've called the police."

Amanda turned into his arms. "What did they say?"

"I have to go down to the station and give them a picture of her and sign a formal statement. After I do that, I'm going out to look for her again."

"I'll come with you."

"No. I need you to wait here in case she calls or comes back." His eyes filled with tears and he pulled Amanda to him. "If anything happens to her..."

"Nothing's going to happen to her," Amanda told him. It couldn't. Taking a steadying breath, she pulled back so

she could see his face. She stroked his jaw with her fingertips, feeling the light stubble that shadowed his face. "We'll
find her, Michael. I know we will."

"I hope you're right." Straightening his shoulders, Michael set Amanda away from him. "I'll call you from the
police station."

He picked up his coat. As he did so, the court petition
envelope fell from the couch to the ground beside the carton.

Amanda stooped down and picked it up. Suddenly her
body went cold. Feeling as though her heart might stop, she
dropped to the floor and started searching for the court
subpoena and hearing notice.

"Amanda, what is it? What's the matter?"

"The notice about the custody hearing," she told him
while frantically shoving aside the carton. She scrambled,
searching under the table.

"What about it?"

"I dropped it in here...on the floor." She started pulling the pillows from the couch and tossing them onto the
floor. "It's not here. I dropped it in here when you called to
me from the study."

Michael paled as her words registered.

"It must have fallen on the floor. And when Summer
came down to get the box..."

Michael sank down onto the couch; he buried his head in
his hands. "No wonder she ran away. She must hate me for
lying to her."

Amanda sat down next to him and squeezed his arm.
"You don't know that. Once you explain to her—"

"Explain what?" he shot back. "That I deliberately kept
her grandmother from her? You know how much she
wanted to find the woman. Would you forgive me if you
were her?"

"Yes," Amanda whispered. She touched his face. "I'd
forgive you because I love you. And Summer loves you,
too."

Michael turned his face into her palm and kissed it. "What would I do without you?"

"You're not going to get a chance to find out. Come on, we've got to call Martha."

But after being told for the third time that Mrs. Winthrop was out, Michael slammed down the telephone receiver. "I'm going over there," he told Amanda. "That damn butler of hers won't tell me anything."

Grabbing her bag, Amanda followed Michael to the door. He pulled it open and nearly ran into Martha Winthrop. She stood on the step with Summer beside her, her hand lifted, poised to knock.

"Summer!" Michael dropped to his knees and reached for his niece. He hugged her to him.

"I'm sorry I left without telling you," Summer said.

"It doesn't matter, kitten. Just as long as you're all right."

"May I come in?" Martha asked, her voice cool.

Michael seemed unable to move, so Amanda stepped forward and touched his shoulder. He stepped back, taking Summer with him.

"Of course, Martha. Come in." Amanda shut the door and went to stand beside Michael and Summer. "Please, sit down," she said, gesturing to a chair.

Martha sat down and for the first time Amanda noted that she looked older, more tired than the last time she'd seen her. The regal bearing was still there, but the proud tilt of her chin wasn't quite as high and her usually squared shoulders had the slightest droop. Even her green eyes seemed to have lost some of their fire.

"In case you're wondering, I didn't kidnap Summer."

"We know that," Amanda said.

"She called me. She told me she knew I was her grandmother and said that she needed to see me. I knew if I told you she'd called, you'd refuse to let me see her. So I told her to wait for me outside."

Summer's eyes were wide, frightened, as she looked at her uncle. "I came down to get the other box, to bring it upstairs. And I heard you and Aunt Mandy shouting at each other. Aunt Mandy said she wasn't going to marry you...because of me...because of the c-custody suit. She said she was going away and not coming back."

Amanda's heart ached at the pain she had caused this child. "Oh, Summer. I'm so sorry you heard that. Those things I said, it wasn't because of you. It was because of *me*. Because *I* was afraid."

"I didn't want you to go away. I was going to unpack your things so you would have to stay. But when I came to get the box, I found this paper." She held out the document and Michael took it. "It said...it said I had a grandmother and that she wanted me to come live with her." Summer sniffed; tears welled in her eyes as she looked at her uncle. "You told me I didn't have a grandmother," she accused.

Michael's face was ashen. "I know," he said, his voice barely audible. "I'm sorry I lied to you, Summer. It was wrong of me."

"Anyway, I got my grandmother's name from that paper and called information. They gave me her number, so I called her."

Tears slid down Amanda's cheeks as she listened to Summer. This was as much her fault as Michael's. Her own fears and insecurities had led to this. And she'd hurt the two people she loved most.

"I know I shouldn't have come here and taken her as I did. I can see by your faces that you were worried. But I won't apologize. No matter how much you dislike it, she *is* my granddaughter." Martha's chin rose proudly. "And if it were up to me, I wouldn't have brought her back."

"Why did you?" Michael asked.

"Because she asked me to." She glanced over at Summer, and Amanda could see the yearning. "As much as I want her to be with me, I want her to be happy even more. I blame myself for her father's unhappiness." She twisted her hands in her lap. "I should have let him marry your sister when he wanted to. If I had, they might both still be alive today. And I wouldn't have lost all these years with my granddaughter."

Her voice cracked and Amanda watched her fight for control. After swallowing, Martha looked directly at Michael. "I know I can give Summer a better life than you can. And if we went to court, I'm sure I could beat you. But I ruined my son's life by forcing him to live by my standards. I'm not going to make the same mistake with my granddaughter. She loves the two of you and wants to be with you. Summer's asked me not to fight you for custody. So I won't. I've already instructed my attorneys to drop the lawsuit."

Martha glanced over at Summer and gave her a small smile. "Come say goodbye to your grandmother, child." She opened her arms and Summer rushed into them.

Amanda nearly choked on the lump in her throat. She reached for Michael's hand.

Martha held Summer a moment longer, then pulled back. She cupped her cheek. "Be happy, dear. And remember, I love you. If you ever want anything, need anything, all you have to do is call."

"I love you, too, Grandma. And I'll remember."

She stood. "Take good care of my granddaughter and make her happy," Martha ordered with a touch of her old arrogance. "Because if you don't, you'll both answer to me." Martha started for the door.

"Martha, wait," Michael called out.

She turned around to face him.

"I...we need to talk."

Amanda squeezed Michael's fingers, realizing how difficult this was for him and trying to give him the strength to continue.

"I'd planned to call you, anyway. I..." He looked at Amanda, then back at Martha. "Amanda's helped me to see how selfish I've been. All these years I've blamed you for my father's death."

Martha sighed. "It was an accident, Michael. And he was the one who opted not to take out adequate insurance for your family."

"I know that. But it was easier to blame you than him. And then when Sara left, I blamed you for that, too."

"If it's any consolation, I hold myself responsible for what happened to her and Phillip."

"It wasn't your fault—not entirely. It was mine, too. Sara may have left because she was afraid you'd take Summer from her, but I'm the reason she stayed away. Because I wouldn't let go of the anger and hatred." He took a deep breath and continued. "I almost lost Summer and the woman I love because I was afraid to give them a choice. I thought if I let Summer know you, love you, that she wouldn't love me."

He looked at Amanda and her heart swelled at the love in his eyes.

"I know now that the only way to hold on to someone's love is by allowing them to give it freely."

He looked back at Martha. "And just because Summer loves you doesn't mean she won't love me. You're her grandmother and you should be a part of her life."

Martha remained silent, her expression closed. But when Summer moved toward her, she opened her arms. She glanced up at Michael. "I don't know what to say, except thank you."

Summer turned to face them. "Does this mean I can go for visits now like Michelle does with her grandmother?"

"Yes, it does," Michael assured her.

"And I can stay overnight?"

"If it's all right with your grandmother," Michael told her.

"It's fine with me. She's welcome anytime."

"How about next week?" Michael asked.

Amanda shot him a puzzled look. "Next week?"

He grinned. "I know Summer and I come as a package deal. But even you have to admit three's a crowd on a honeymoon." He looked over at Martha. "Would you mind keeping Summer for a week while Amanda and I go on a honeymoon?"

Martha smiled; her eyes brimmed with tears. "Take two weeks, take a month, if you'd like."

"Wait till I tell Michelle," Summer said excitedly, then followed it with a big yawn.

Amanda chuckled. "I think Michelle's going to have to wait until tomorrow. It's time you got ready for bed. We've got a lot to do before Saturday." She looked up at Martha. "Would you like to tuck her in?"

"I'd like that. Very much," Martha said.

"Come on, Grandma, I'll show you my room." Taking her by the hand, Summer led the older woman up the stairs.

Once they were alone, Michael took Amanda in his arms. "No second thoughts?"

She snuggled closer. "About what?"

"Marrying me." He paused. "I come with a lot of baggage, Amanda. I'm stubborn..."

"True."

"And impatient..."

"I know."

"And I have a tendency to force my will upon other people."

"Yes, you do."

"I know I practically forced you into agreeing on a quick wedding, when I should probably have let you have the engagement you wanted."

"I don't want a long engagement, Michael."

"And I guess I'm selfish, too, because I don't want to give you more time when I know I should. But I'm too afraid of losing you," he said.

"Michael, are you listening to me? I don't want more time." She slid her arms around his neck.

"You don't?"

"No." She brushed her lips across his. "I love you. And I want to marry you. On Saturday."

"You do?" he asked, his voice growing husky.

"Mmm-hmm." She traced his mouth with her tongue. A thrill of excitement went through her as Michael pressed his body, already hard with desire, against her. "You weren't the only one who was afraid, Michael. I was afraid, too. Afraid to take a chance on loving you."

"And now?"

"I'm still afraid, but I know now that loving you and being loved by you is worth any risk."

* * * * *

Another wonderful year of romance
concludes with

Christmas Memories

Share in the magic and memories of romance
during the holiday season with this collection of two
full-length contemporary Christmas stories,
by two bestselling authors

Diana Palmer
Marilyn Pappano

Available in December at your favorite retail outlet.

Only from

Silhouette®

where passion lives.

presents

WATCHING FOR WILLA
by Helen R. Myers

Willa's new neighbor was watching her.
Her every move, her every breath. With his
mysterious past, Zachary Denton was an
enigma. He claimed he only wanted to
warn her, protect her—possess her. And
like a butterfly drawn into a deadly web,
Willa could not resist his mesmerizing
sensual pull.

But was he a loving protector—or a
scheming predator?

Find out this February—only from
Silhouette Shadows.

SSHRM

THE BRANIGANS ARE BACK!

You fell in love with the rugged Branigan brood
before—now those brothers have returned...
sexier than ever!

Coming in January from

BRANIGAN'S BREAK by Leslie Davis Guccione

Irresistible Sean Branigan didn't need help raising his
two teenagers—especially from beautiful Julia Hollins!
She was driving him crazy with all her advice...*and*
with her sinfully sexy ways!

Don't miss BRANIGAN'S BREAK (#902) by
Leslie Davis Guccione—only from Silhouette Desire.

HOMETOWN WEDDING
by Pamela Macaluso

Don't miss JUST MARRIED!, a fun-filled new series by
Pamela Macaluso about three men with wealth, power and
looks to die for. These bad boys had everything—except the
love of a good woman.

Bad boy Rorke O'Neil has all the local women's hearts
racing. Yet Callie Harrison had learned the hard way
just what a wild, worldly hellion Rorke really is...but
how can she forget how wonderful it felt to be in his big,
strong arms?

Find out in *Hometown Wedding*, coming to you in
December...only from

JM

Is the future what it's cracked up to be?

This December, discover what commitment is all about in

GETTING ATTACHED: CJ
by Wendy Corsi Staub

C. J. Clarke was tired of lugging her toothbrush around town, and she sure didn't believe longtime boyfriend David Griffin's constant whining about "not being able to commit." He was with her every day—and most nights—so what was his problem? C.J. knew marriage wasn't always what it was cracked up to be, but when you're in love you're supposed to end up happily ever after...aren't you?

The ups and downs of life as you know it continue with

GETTING A LIFE: MARISSA
by Kathryn Jensen (January)

GETTING OUT: EMILY
by ArLynn Presser (February)

Get smart. Get into "The Loop"!